NOLA Gals

by

Barbara J. Rebbeck

Neverland Publishing Company
Miami, FL

This book is a work of fiction. References to real people, events, establishments, organization, or locales are intended only to provide a sense of authenticity and are used to advance the fictional narrative. All other characters, and all incidents and dialogue, are drawn from the author's imagination and are not intended to be considered real or factual.

Copyright © 2014 by Barbara J. Rebbeck

All rights reserved, including the right of reproduction in whole or in part in any form.

Cover Design by Joe Font

Library of Congress Control Number: 2014958770

Printed in the United States of America

ISBN: 978-0-9903148-68

www.neverlandpublishing.com

For my sister, Mary
the oldest
And my brother, Dave
the youngest.
Both gone far too soon
And both missed every day.

For Russ who came to my birthday party in second grade, the only little boy with twenty-one girls!

Barbara J. Bebbeck

"It's bad children like you makes the seasons change."

To Kill a Mockingbird

Harper Lee

ESSENCE

Essence trudged down the street along the mighty Mississippi in the grueling August heat. The sky was cloudless, the wind absent. Things looked just fine to her. What was all the jibber-jabber about anyway?

"Hurry up, child," her grandmother, Mimmi, called back to her. Little Chardonnai was perched on her left hip, her skinny legs wrapping round. A plastic bag of groceries rode her right hip, another bag, hanging from her hand. Chardonnai was losing a battle with a cherry Popsicle as it melted faster than she could lick it, all down the messy stick now a grainy red. The red drips splotched down Mimmi's old sun-flowered sundress. "We have got to get this food home fast before it spoils in the sun. Essence, give that old George a boot to move his butt along. He's about to get on my last nerve."

Essence twisted around, peering over the bags she carried only to see George at his usual slow pace, poking at the iron gates of each house along the road, nosy as ever. "George," she yelled,

NOLA Gals/Barbara J. Rebbeck

"get yourself up here. Ain't nothing in these houses for your skinny old self. No ladies' dainties or gentlemen's whities." George turned his head and made a leisurely effort to catch up with her. Nothing to break a sweat. He was a funny old dog, a French poodle, but not the kind you see in fancy magazines—the little cute ones with small bows in their perfectly cut hairdos prancing along on a leash beside some high-class lady. No, this poodle was big, but so skinny he looked like a skeleton. And he was stuuuupid as could be. When he stood up on his hind legs, you'd swear he was some old French monsieur. The kind who was poor, but still proud. He came up to Essence's shoulders and towered over little Chardonnai.

"Wish we had a car," Essence complained to George who was now loping alongside of her.

"No good wishin' for impossible things," Mimmi shouted back at her. Another of her "truths," as she called them. Essence had a million of her grandmother's bits of wisdom to live by. Maybe one of them wise knowings could help them now with a bad hurricane on the way.

As they passed by house after house, Essence began to feel more and more uneasy. Nearly every household was a shambles as the families who lived all along the Mississippi were packing, boarding up the windows and doors, preparing to leave.

"Little girl," a man called to her as he loaded an old suitcase into his truck, "you'd best be telling your old grandmama to get you packed and out of here. Katrina is on her way, and she's sure to stir up this old pot of gumbo once more. She's a mean old gal."

"You tell her. She says we'll be okay and she's not letting some old storm take our house." A little boy about six ran out of the house, carrying a bulky bag of toys to the car.

"You can't take all this," his dad yelled. "What are you thinking, child? Here, take this," he said, pulling a tattered teddy bear out of the bag. The little kid started to cry and stared at Essence as if she could help save his treasures. "Just get in the car, son," his dad called, sighing as he tossed the whole bag in the trunk.

"Essence, girl, what you dawdling for now?" Mimmi's voice interrupted. "Get your butt moving. Faster, girl."

But Essence knew leaving was near to impossible—as impossible as getting that new car. Old Mimmi loved the 9th Ward here in New Orleans. She adored the cool sounds of Satchmo and Fats Domino; the rich diet of shrimp and okra gumbo, rum raisin French toast, and crawfish pie; the walks along the Industrial Canal when the sun slipped into shade. She looked ahead at the old lady, almost stomping in that determined gait of hers. Head high, sweat dripping down her cheeks under the old straw bonnet, those extra pounds bumping up and down her hips, further weighed down with groceries and her grandchild, Chardonnai. Unafraid, Mimmi began to sing her favorite song about that lazy old river. Essence recognized that old Louis Armstrong song in Mimmi's rich tones at once. How many evenings had she spent listening to the old record scratching its music into the night air? Mimmi half-turned back to her and tossed her a "truth" from Mr. Armstrong himself. "Satchmo Armstrong, now there's a wise man. He said that this city has given him something to live for. Amen! Amen! We're not going anywhere. I love this old noon sun too much."

"No, ma'am. We'll be staying on," Essence agreed. George's ears perked up at Satchmo's song as they walked along. But Essence had always had other plans as she first watched the Mississippi rolling its way—away—to anywhere, but here. She dreamed of finding her daddy and living good. All she knew about her daddy was that he was a musician like Mr. Armstrong—maybe with a funny nickname like Satchmo, too. Mimmi said her daddy could play a trumpet so the notes dripped over you like hot molasses. But she added fast that molasses wasn't thick enough to stick for long at all. No, sir, not good enough for her daughter. Should have been sticky glue 'cause that man—her daddy—had lifted his butt onto those sweet trumpet notes of his and vanished up some lazy river, leaving Essence, Chardonnai, and her mother with Mimmi and skinny old George. Now what would happen to them because of this stubborn old lady? She was all they had.

As they moved closer to home, Essence knew that this old white house was the reason they would stay. Generations of their family had lived here in this house, built in the 1800s from wood from the barges that had originally carried coal down the river to the city. Mimmi had made her learn its history by heart—that this house was a "single shotgun" design, meaning if you looked down the house from inside the front door, you could see the back door—a single shot. They neared the porch and Essence saw their neighbors walking down the street the other way. It seemed like everyone was going the other way. Everyone but them.

"Billy." Essence shouted to her best friend, "Where you going?"

"The mayor is sending buses," he called back. "They'll take us to the Superdome."

"Oh, no," Mimmi interrupted, "we're not going to roast in that huge stadium. We'll be just fine here. You'll see. Been through this all before. All before."

Essence watched as Billy, weighed down by a black plastic bag flung over his shoulder, followed behind his mom. He struggled to keep up, his short legs pumping in his old denim shorts and flip-flops. George ran at him and near tackled him, barking a fierce goodbye. They were good pals, Billy and her dog, George. They'd spent long hours goofing around together on walks along the river. Billy loved to toss an old yellow tennis ball, and George would run fast and retrieve it, charging back to Billy. They'd practiced enough in the lazy summer heat that sometimes George would leap into the air and catch the ball right in his mouth. Essence would giggle and laugh, hoping George would bring the wet ball back to her. Sometimes he would hold on to it with his teeth and she would pry open his jaws to get it. Other times he'd drop it at her feet, all sloppy wet while he rubbed up against her leg. Even though Billy was a couple years younger than her, she and Billy talked a lot about their families. Mimmi said they were confidants. She knew he didn't like his stepfather much, and it had been real hard for him when his mom got married again after his real dad died in Iraq. He showed her the medals he kept under his pillow. Every night he polished them, spitting on them and then rubbing them with an old tie his dad had worn when he married his mom. "At least you got a daddy in your house," she kept reminding him. "My daddy is out there somewhere on the loose, Mimmi says."

"Goodbye, George," Billy called back. "I'll miss you." He knelt down on the pavement and gave old George a hug. As he did, his jacket fell open and Essence could see the gleam of something metal pressed against his chest. *The medals*, she thought.

"Bye," he called to Essence.

"Get over here, George," Mimmi shouted. "No reason to say goodbye. They'll be back. All this packing and buses. Just ridiculous," she fumed. Stopping to take a break, and heaving a sigh, Mimmi lifted the groceries and Chardonnai onto the porch, shaking her head, turning away from Billy and his panicky ways.

"Bye, be safe," Essence called back. Billy had told her these were the last words his dad had ever said to him. Tears started to form, and she quickly tried to pull them back so Mimmi wouldn't see and call her a weak baby-child. Mimmi wouldn't cotton to no tears ever.

Climbing up the porch steps behind her grandmama, Essence knew it was hopeless. She wished Pippi was still alive. He might be able to budge the old woman. She could just hear him pointing out to her the three hand-carved brackets that held the small roof above the porch, the fine workmanship of the iron gate on the walkway. But surely he wouldn't have risked his grandbabies' lives. He would have loved them more than this old NOLA house. New Orleans, Louisiana. No, sir. His girls would come first.

Chardonnai, climbing down from Mimmi's hip, landed with a bump, and said, "Can I go through the window? Please, Mimmi? Tell me the story. Tell me the story."

"Like we got time for stories. You tell her," Mimmi said to Essence, banging her way through the door with the bags. "I'll go open the window so we get some air in the house before the storm gets roaring."

"Okay," Essence said, none too happy. She sat down on the old wicker chair and pulled Chardonnai onto her lap, trying to ignore the parade of neighbors passing by. Chardonnai looked up at her, concentrating hard on every word.

NOLA Gals/Barbara J. Rebbeck

"In the olden days in France," she began, "the poor folks got real mad at the rich ones who lived in fancy castles so they had a big revolution and chopped the rich guys' heads off on a guillotine. They made this evil machine and named it Ma'am Guillotine. She was a mean old gal who chopped heads off with a wicked, sharp blade that dropped on their necks and lopped their heads off like they were cabbages. But first they had to stay in jail and take off their powder wigs and get haircuts so the blade could find their necks easier. They rode to the square in town in carts, climbed up rickety stairs, and knelt down. Whoosh! That old Ma'am Guillotine sliced their head clean off. And an ugly old soldier held it up all dripping with blood to the crowd. They cheered and hooted real loud. So they named these ten-foot windows on our porches guillotines because they rise and fall just like those old sharp blades."

With that Chardonnai rose on her toes, giggled, bowed to Essence and danced herself through the window that was level with the porch floor. *Silly girl*, Essence thought. *Doesn't she realize she just got her head chopped off?* But who knew how long all their heads would be above water? She envied Chardonnai being too young to get what was heading her way. Essence knew she needed to protect her. That was a truth.

Standing on the porch, Essence remembered that her grandpa hadn't liked music much at all. He'd often called himself the only old man in New Orleans who couldn't carry a tune, not even in a bucket to the Mississippi. But when he died, Mimmi had said that he had left her just well off enough with this house. Another Mimmi-truth was born. "You can buy music on a record, in a jazz club, in a church, but you can't buy yourself a good man. Remember that, Essence Lafontaine." So when her daddy poof-vanished, her mama had said, "Hope I never hear notes off a trumpet again. That man was useless for us girls. Essence, stay clear of any man who's gonna play you jazz. Those hot notes slippery like molasses got no backbone, just like your daddy, Harold."

With that, the music had stopped. All Essence had left now was a photo of a handsome man holding a shiny trumpet in his right hand, a smile cracking his dark face with laughter. She'd found it in an old suitcase in a trunk in the shed when they'd first moved in. The only reason she'd known who it was was the name *Harold* printed on the back in swirly handwriting. She'd hidden it under her mattress knowing her mama would rip it up if she saw it. Every night she'd take it out, close her eyes and wish on it. She knew that man in the photo must be living good, playing good, and just waiting to come get her—to show her the good times, buy her beads for Mardi Gras, feed her fine French cuisine, and let her live with him in an elegant mansion in the French Quarter. She'd sit on the balcony, lean over the iron railing, careful not to lose her beads, and listen, just close her eyes and listen as that hot molasses dripped ever so slowly into a soothing lazy river of love—love just for her, Harold's daughter, Essence Lafontaine.

"Last nerve," she heard Mimmi call. "Yes, indeed, you girls are on my last nerve."

GRACE

Grace stopped singing her favorite Carrie Underwood tune in mid-sentence as her mom tapped her on the forehead in that annoying listen-to-me gesture. Pulling the iPod bud from her ear, Grace sighed, "What now? You're only interrupting her heaven song." For effect, she rolled her eyes and slumped back into the soft quilt on her bed, staring at the painting on the wall. The Degas ballet dancer ignored her, engaged in an elegant plié.

"You'd think you'd be sick of Carrie Underwood by now," her mother said, "It's been a summer since she won *American Idol*."

"I'm one of Carrie's Care Bears, forever loyal," Grace replied, hoping this would send her mother back to wherever she'd come from. Probably cleaning some dog kennel. Pushing back further into the pillows, she attempted to listen to the song again, but her mom caught her hand.

"Well, some of us have to work, my lovely Grace."

"Not me. I've got just a few days left before school starts. I'm exhausted from just getting my uniform."

"Poor dear. I still haven't gotten the credit card bills from your trip to San Antonio for the Idol Tour Concert."

"Mom, that was so the best night of my life. To see Carrie live, I mean..."

"Well, your dad and I felt you had earned that trip. We know last year was tough for you," she replied as she turned and headed down the stairs.

"Ya think?" Grace broke in, jumping up from the bed to follow. "I only had to get used to a totally—and I mean totally—new school."

"And whose fault was that?" her mom asked, sighing, hoping the argument would not start again as Grace thumped behind her down the stairs.

But Grace grabbed the bone again like a hungry dog, "You made me leave LBJ Middle School. I had no choice."

"That's right. There was no choice. You had broken every rule and been suspended too many times." Her mother turned on the stairs to look Grace full in the face.

"So you locked me up in a convent!" Grace said, each word accented for dramatic effect. She glared at her mom.

"It had to be done. Coming home from a party at three a.m. on a school night. The drinking, smoking. Your grades in the toilet." Her mom turned and continued down the stairs and reached the table in the foyer and bustled about gathering her bag and keys.

"But I changed. I really tried." Grace countered, following her to the door. "I knelt down in the chapel and let everybody stare at the new sinner from the evil public school."

"Yes, you did. I only hope you can keep it up this year so you can get to high school in one piece."

Grace looked away. Life wasn't that bad, but she'd rather die than admit that. Yes, life was just fine here in River Oaks. She really had been proud to bring her new friend, Lindsey, home to this house in the suburbs, an easy ride into Houston. The house was a graceful New-Orleans style home as her mom called it. Odd to have a Louisiana style house in Texas. She'd made friends with Lindsey just a few weeks into her exile at St.

NOLA Gals/Barbara J. Rebbeck

Catherine's. She was a good friend and willing to take a few risks. Never boring, that's for sure. Lindsey's stepmom and dad were a bit of a scandal. Her dad had dumped Lindsey's mom for a "new model," the girls joked. Lindsey hated her new mom. She called her "Super," embarrassingly short for superficial. It was a joke that went over her stepmom's head as she often told people how special she felt that Lindsey regarded her as "super." Her dad had set off fireworks when he had tried to have his first marriage to Lindsey's mom annulled so he could stay a good Catholic. "And what would that have made me?" Lindsey had asked Grace. "Invisible? Unborn? Annulled?" In the end, he'd settled for a divorce, but the damage had been done.

"Are you sure you don't want to come to the clinic for just a little while?" her mom asked.

Grace hesitated for a moment; she did love to pet and pamper all those little guys, especially the sick ones at the clinic. But instead she walked over and sank into the comfy couch. Listening to the air conditioner humming against the Texas heat, she nodded her head in an exaggerated no, you've-got-to-be-kiddin' response. It was just too hot. Her mom, Dr. Woodson, was one of the best vets in Houston, and Grace had spent many hours this summer helping out. She adored the squiggly little puppies and kitties, their pitiful eyes begging for a soothing rub or quick kiss, especially when they were drowsy after surgery. But enough was enough. School loomed, and she was secretly looking forward to her last year at St. Catherine's Middle School for Girls or "Cat's" as they all called it. She'd be content just snuggling with her new little kitty, Idol, for the morning. After persuading her parents that it was very odd to have a petless vet for a mom, they'd relented to her pleas for a kitty. Days later, she had brought home a little ball of white long-haired fuzz from the clinic.

"Your dad has a heavy load of patients today so you'll be mostly on your own," her mom continued, giving the room a once-around inspection.

Grace stood up and walked through the French doors to the patio. Maybe she could lie in the sun. No, she reconsidered as she hopped on the hot tiles from foot to foot, her bare feet burning.

"That's okay," she called back to her mother. "I'll go to Lindsey's for lunch." A lunch without dog or people problems would be great and it was Super's day at the spa. When your mom's a vet and your dad's a psychiatrist sometimes you just crave a little talk about TV or movies, neither of which her parents had time for. They just didn't appreciate shows like Idol. In fact, the only way Grace had been able to go see the Idol tour had been to agree to see a production of *Romeo and Juliet* last spring by the Houston Ballet. They had read the play in school, actually laughing all the way as girls played all the parts including the famous lovers. Dancers from the ballet had come to school before they saw the performance and explained it all. Grace would never admit it or tell her parents, but she had loved every second of it.

"And eat some meat. You need protein."

"But..."

"I know. Carrie is a vegetarian."

Now she'd gone too far. Grace slammed through the doors and flew back into the living room, her bare toes curling into the thick carpet. Ignoring her mother, she stomped across the room to the stairs and launched herself to the hall upstairs. *This house is just too French*, she thought as she gazed at the bedroom doors surrounding her. The hallway was all done in blue and yellow. "Country French," her mom called it. Just the word *French* upset Grace as Sister Grenier had become her mortal enemy at school. There weren't too many nuns left at the school, but it was just Grace's luck to have two of the deadliest for classes. Sister Grenier had been her nemesis when she first began the study of the French language—the tongue of the great royalty in history— the language of the Sun King—the jewel in the crown. Oui, oui. Yeah, yeah. All it meant to Grace was standing and reciting endless verbs in their stupid tenses. Borrrrring! Unfortunately for Sister Grenier, all the girls knew that her name translated close to "frog" so she received an ovation of croaks wherever she went, of course behind her back. If they'd ever meet a few cute *garçons*, it would be more interesting. But just conjugating the verb "to love" didn't do it for Grace and her *amies*. Last year Grace had come up with her successful system of buckling down just a few weeks before quarterly parent conferences. No sass, lots of Yes, Sister, and droning verbs steered her through rough waters. And she was not above using the nuns' poor-girl-saved-from-the-public-school mission to extend their patience with her. "But Sister," Grace could plead, "I'm trying to adjust to goals and values that are so new to me. I'm bound to make mistakes." Sometimes she even cried, her acting skills improving faster than her conscience.

"And do that summer reading." Her mom's final farewell drifted up the stairs behind her as Grace looked around her room. Carrie Underwood smiled at her in various poses from the posters on the walls, her smile assuring Grace that she understood her. Grace moved to her oak desk and opened her laptop. She always thought about her Grandpa Woodson when she sat at this old desk. It had been his. She had loved to sit at it on his lap and find that secret compartment. She ran her hands over the smooth surface now, remembering his ocean-blue eyes and his long hands. She remembered him at parades clapping so hard with his big hands whenever the veterans marched by. This desk was all she had left of him. He had left it to her with a letter and photo hidden in the secret drawer. She pulled the photo out and stared at her granddad, smiling in his air force uniform. She missed him.

Checking her email, she knew she had no time to blog now. She'd work on her forbidden page at Lindsey's. Her parents were really clueless to hi-tech. The "Doctor Duo," as Grace called her parents, had read an article in the Times about the evils of such pages. She could remember them sitting on the patio, sipping their latest favorite cocktails, pomegranate something-or-others, shocked at the creeps who preyed on these sites. They then had made sure all the nuns and teachers saw the article, and the boom had been lowered on all the girls. Absolutely no MySpace pages for Cat's ladies. Of course, word had gotten out that it had been the Doctor Duo behind the total ban so Grace had not been too popular there for a while. So she and Lindsey had gone underground. They'd spent hours yesterday with their digital cameras, posing for just the right photos for their pages. No Catholic plaid uniform here. They needed just the right color tops; blue for Lindsey's eyes, green for Grace. Posing in a million different ways all morning, trying to look older and a little sexy, perhaps a bit hotter than Carrie would approve of, they had finally loved the two faces smiling back at them from the screen.

Life was good, Grace thought as she plopped her iPod into the dock on a shelf on her media center and headed towards her walk-in closet. What to wear for a scorching Houston day? She began to sing along at the top of her lungs with Carrie.

ESSENCE

"Come on, girl. Wake up from your daydreams and get George into the shed before the rains come." Mimmi appeared in the guillotine window, having unpacked all her groceries. She was dabbing away at a Popsicle stain on her worn house dress with an old washcloth.

"Come on, stuuuupid," Essence yanked at George's leash, pulled him off the porch and around the side of the house to the old shed. Essence could see right into the kitchen next door. They were all hustling around, packing food while Mr. Jackson prepared to board up their guillotine window from the outside. He leaned over their porch before Essence could reach the shed.

"Essence, if your grandmama is too silly to leave, at least maybe she'll let you girls come with us to the Superdome."

Essence knew it was useless even to think about. "No, we'll be all right, Mr. Jackson. Thanks for asking."

She opened the door to the shed, and for once, George went in willingly, probably glad to get out of the sun, even as stupid as he was. Closing the door, she jumped as Chardonnai's little wading pool whooshed up into the air, smacking into the shed, deflating like a lumpy, plastic marshmallow. Essence looked up, wondering just what powerful force was on its way.

"Mimmi," she yelled into the kitchen window, "how long before Mama gets home from work?"

"Hush, child, the mayor is on TV. He's giving us all advice on this storm."

Essence hurried into the house. Chardonnai had begun to cry. They grabbed each other and ran into Mimmi's arms. All three sat on the sagging couch, watching and listening, Mimmi's strong arms around them both. The mayor and the governor were telling everyone to evacuate, to leave the city. "We are facing the storm most of us have feared," the mayor stated. Chardonnai began to wail even louder.

"Well, Mister Mayor," Mimmi snapped back at the screen, "just how am I supposed to leave this city? In my shiny limo? By private jet?"

"But Mimmi..."

"Only butts I want to hear or see are ours staying right here in our home. They always tell big whopper lies about these storms. You'll see. We survived Betsy, Andrew and that old devil, Ivan. No, we're not going." She hugged the girls closer to her. "Why, I can hear your hearts beating fast, my gals. Don't you worry. Your mama should be home soon."

Essence pushed her way up from Mimmi's hug, got up from the couch, and looked out the guillotine window. What could she possibly do to change that old woman's mind? Outside it still looked peaceful. Hard to believe what they were predicting. Maybe they would be all right after all.

"Essence, you'd best get that old dog back out of the shed. I can hear him yowling. Must sense the rain that's coming. If floods come, we'll move on up to the second floor to your mama's room. You'll see. We'll be all right. We'll use this old house like the Ark old Noah built. Too bad George doesn't have a wife. Two by two." She laughed and gave Chardonnai a kiss, hugging her hard against her.

NOLA Gals/Barbara J. Rebbeck

Essence knew Mimmi was trying to be funny, but no one was laughing now.

More news came from the TV, repeating what the man on the road had told her. The mayor was sending buses to get people over to the Superdome. You had to walk a ways, but they'd find you. They would get you out. Promise.

"No, no," Mimmi answered back to the TV. "You're not stuffing these old bones in some football arena. We'll be just fine on our own. Betsy didn't get us, and no way will that Katrina gal."

Essence ran out to the shed and found George had quit howling and was munching on an old pair of silky underpants. *Oh, no*, she thought, *he's at the dainties again*. For some reason he loved a good pair of undies. How he managed to swallow them whole mystified Essence and set Char to giggling. Mimmi said some day he'd get a blockage and die, but nothing would stop his appetite for nasty panties. "Come on, George. Drop those panties," Essence coached. "Got to move you to higher ground. Then I gotta go get that photo of my daddy out from under the mattress. Whatever happens now, I need my daddy near." George took one last chew on the undies, let them fall, and followed Essence across the yard. He stopped midway to the porch, stood on his hind legs, stretched his neck and yowled at the sky. Essence shivered. Even stupid George knew Katrina was on her way.

GRACE

Grace hated Sunday mornings, especially this one, the first Sunday liturgy for the new school year. Not that her family went to church often. Her mom and dad usually took Sunday literally as "a day of rest," easing up, relaxing with the newspapers over coffee on the patio, discovering articles that would get Grace in trouble with all her friends, while she herself slept in. They tended to leave the religious side of life to the school and their required liturgies and religion classes, although they had paid more attention since Grace had switched from the public school. Grace stood in the foyer, dressed in her new uniform, hot, hot, hot, awaiting inspection. As an eighth grader, she had graduated to a navy blue blazer with her blue plaid skirt and knee socks. Standing there, in Lindsey's color, she was melting fast, even in the air conditioning.

"We may as well do the pop-can test here before church," her dad said, half-mocking, half-serious.

"Do I have to?" Grace replied, hating this stupid ritual.

NOLA Gals/Barbara J. Rebbeck

"Oh, it looks okay, the right length," said her mom, joining them in the foyer, "but better be sure."

Grace knelt down on the tile floor which at least felt cool to her knees. She looked up at her mom who stooped to place a pop can in front of her knees below the hemline of her skirt. Yes, the skirt just barely skimmed the top of the can. She was safe, legal, her skirt a respectful length that is until she rolled it up around the waist once away from watchful eyes. Grace knew better than to voice her opinion on such stupid, borrrring games. Her opinion didn't matter. At least her parents had yet to discover her MySpace page. If Sister Margaret knew, she would send her to confession at once to atone for this most mortal of sins. Grace had laughed at the sinister letter her parents had received yesterday, warning all the good little girls of St. Catherine's once more about the evils of technology and the perverted predators who were waiting to pounce on their innocence in their wireless but sinful communications. Her parents had seized upon the letter as a way to squeeze in one more back-to-school lecture on behavior and consequences. She and Lindsey had laughed about it as she had heard almost the same lecture word for word from her dad, a lawyer who *knew* all the legal consequences.

"Your mom approves of your skirt so your carriage awaits, Princess Grace," her dad laughed, putting his arm around her. She was already sweating under her navy blazer and those knee socks were ridiculous on August 28th. She looked at her mom, wishing she could have worn a light summer dress like the green one she had on. Just her color, not Mom's. And now she had to sit through a liturgy. She had thought about sneaking her iPod under her long, dark hair, but the heat was melting her rebellious spirit into a puddle of sweat.

"Come on," her mother said, nudging her in the back. "You look perfect. We'll show up, smile, pray, sing, give a donation, and then it's off to the Club for brunch. Maybe there'll be some cute guys. And tonight, you read your novel."

Dripping her way down the driveway to the car, Grace said, "Oh, yeah, and I'm such a looker in this outfit. The guys will love these socks."

"But there will be a/c," added her dad, feeling a bit sorry for his over-heated daughter as he opened the back door of the Cadillac for her.

Grace's mom slid into the front seat as her dad walked around to the driver's side. "Grace, I'm very serious. You have got to finish reading *To Kill a Mockingbird.*"

"Oh, yeah. I'll be like Atticus, the lawyer in it, and walk around in someone else's skin, hopefully in air conditioning and Prada shoes. Air. Fast," pleaded Grace from the back, thoroughly absorbed with her own agony.

"Grace," her mom said, trying to divert her attention, "aren't the trees lovely? I think we made the right choices, don't you?"

"I guess so," Grace mumbled looking around the sweep of the circular drive. The names of the trees she'd learned when she had *helped* Troy, their landscape designer plan the front yard, flashed by her in a blur as her dad circled the drive. Sweet Gum, Pecan, Magnolia, Eucalyptus and her favorite, Chinese Parasol. She remembered reviewing all the photos of possible trees when she was so little in a big book Troy had shown her. The book was so large he had to hold it up for her and show her each page, turning back and forth as she mulled over each and then decided. Tony had written down all her choices and some had even made it to the final plantings. She remembered the row of deep holes and the burlap bagged trees, each one maneuvered into the ground and covered with the moist earth. She had worn her flowered gloves and followed behind with her plastic pail of dirt and green metal shovel. She stood back as each tree was planted, and then moved in for a final series of pats. For weeks after, she appeared every day with her daisy-covered watering can and gave each tree a big drink. Grandpa Woodson had accompanied her on her morning garden duties, pointing out to her many gardening secrets, sifting the soil through his long fingers.

"Yes, ma'am," her dad snapped, "Time for music. I loved *Mockingbird*. It won the Pulitzer."

"Lindsey's dad says it's very unrealistic."

"But he's a lawyer, dear," Grace's mom countered.

Oh, great. Music, thought Grace, dreading what tunes would float back to her. She had left Carrie at home on her iPod. Sure enough, something dreadful and classical assaulted her ears.

But then a bulletin broke in. Something about a hurricane and New Orleans. *Cool breezes and rain would feel so good right about now*, Grace thought. Even in the air of the car, she felt stifled. She'd trade a storm anywhere for hot old Houston this Sunday.

"That doesn't sound good at all," Grace's dad said.

"Those things usually change course. It'll be all right," her mom replied.

"But a category five," her dad said, worried in his psychiatrist way.

In a few minutes, they pulled up into the pebbled driveway of St. Catherine's Chapel. Grace looked out the window, stretching every minute she had left in the coolness of the car. She glanced at the stained-glass windows, depicting various saints and then at a group of eighth graders gathered outside the huge carved doors, Lindsey among them. She seemed just as miserable, but brightened when she saw Grace. These were her new friends. In the past year she'd fought hard for acceptance. She'd walked a thin line between the nuns' and her parents' rules and the Cat's girls. She'd tried not to be too good. She'd wanted to be one of the girls. To be able to spend time at their homes, lie out by their pools, shop at the exclusive mall they loved, share their secrets, be their confidante. It was so important to her. And she'd made it. As her dad opened the car door for her, Grace thought that this would be their year. Saints be praised and Sisters beware! "Lindsey," she yelled.

KATRINA

*S*he dips her toe into the ocean off the West African shore, peering out to sea, her white dress billowing around her like a silken sail. She has come on the winds from the hot, thirsty Sahara. Restless, she pulls back, shaking loose the scant beads of water from her shimmering leg. Stooping, she runs her fingers through the rough sand, reaching for a seashell. It has been worn by tentacles of wind, sand and ocean, caressing and lapping round their sinewy fingers, eroding it to a dull roughness. She runs her fingers along the hard crescent shell, turning it to reveal its curled inward cup. Scraping her long, red nails across it, she removes small clumps of errant sand from its spindly surface. Shaking it, and banging it with her flat fist, she dumps more sand from the cup. Pulling it to her ear, she listens as centuries of whispers from the sea call to her, sirens luring her on.

She looks again to the horizon, clear of life, clear of cloud, clear of destiny.

"Mother, I shall leave this place. I shall be free." Her voice raises as the wind increases its roar in competition. Spinning, twirling, she lifts into the air, dropping the shell beneath her. Looking down to the wet sand

NOLA Gals/Barbara J. Rebbeck

below, even she is amazed at her levitation. What magician is at play? How her mother would be jealous.

Flushed with possibility, she moves out over the ocean, her anger rising with her body. Suddenly, she reverses her motion seaward, dropping to the shore once more. She needs the seashell now. As she stoops to retrieve it, grasping it in her right hand, it turns on its own, squirming in her palm, tearing slight cuts as it begins to glow an ashen pink. She holds the shell with her left hand, clamping the right over, and rises again into the darkening air. Ominous clouds are surging over the water, sealing their forces in a counter-clockwise spin. The ocean below begins a slow churn as the clouds blacken the air, eclipsing the sun. The clouds suck vapor off the steaming water, reveling in the moist heat, swelling their cheeks.

Now she would have her way. Soaring upward, she takes her rightful place, dead center in the black clouds. Raising the seashell before her at shoulder height, she points it towards the horizon. A divining rod of sorts, it will guide her to freedom, she knows.

For days she rides above the Atlantic, on a powerful tropical wave growing in size and strength, the seashell guiding her. Over the Bahamas, she sucks up the hot waters, quenches her thirst, and moves on towards Florida. There she slows a bit, curious to see this new land beneath her, amused at her power to bend the palm trees perpendicular and flood the streets with torrential rain. But then, bored, she crosses back over water, howling and spinning over the Gulf of Mexico. Hair in her eyes, lost in dizziness, she holds the seashell up as best she can. Jagged memories of her mother and their fights cut her mind, fueling her determination. She will have her way. She dives like a manic seagull, hovering above the surface of the Gulf, her hand reaching down, skimming the surface, filling the seashell with the moist, hot water. Soaring upward, she cups the seashell gently, careful not to spill.

Guided to the northwest, in command of the waters and the clouds, she becomes nature, her anger propelling her over the city of New Orleans. She swirls, caught up in the vortex of the storm, clasping the seashell tightly to her chest. Her dress, once slick and twisted across her body, parachutes out around her, puffed against the driving rain. She spins, a vein of white marble in the circling black clouds. Laughing, she pushes the seashell out before her and tips it, unleashing a torrent of rain—a surge of water on the helpless city below her. Roaring into the winds, she rants, "Hear me! I am Katrina."

GRACE

Sister Margaret barreled down the computer lab aisle, her eyes squinted almost shut in pursuit, her St. Catherine's polo shirt snug across her ample chest, her hips barely squeezing by the computers. She was a huge tiger stalking, her gel pen and grade book ready. On the prowl, her hair splayed flat over her forehead in the heat, her grim tight lips just waiting for one girl to reveal the forbidden fruit on her screen.

"Everyone," she said, "is reading the article on Colonial America. Say it, ladies. What are you reading?"

"The article on Colonial America," the ladies mumbled.

"So help me, Saint Catherine."

Mumble, mumble. No eye contact, heads down in a prayer not to get caught. She continued down the aisle, almost to Grace and Lindsey. Exchanging a glance at each other, and then at their screens for a last look at MySpace and their faces smiling back, the girls hit the control-w keys, and their screens dissolved into the serious faces of settlers in 1640. *Borrrrring*, Grace thought. But

NOLA Gals/Barbara J. Rebbeck

better to get this history stuff done than be caught doing something fun. No one had yet tested the new zero-tolerance policy on Space pages. The ladies expected someone to be busted at any time. Sister Margaret was relentless. She spent her free time, it was rumored, scrolling through these evil pages, eyes riveted, eager to trap the first offenders. The girls were sure she relished the thought of a public humiliation. Perhaps, taking a cue from the colonists, she would have stocks constructed in the courtyard and stand gloating as the first young lady was locked in, the offending hands denied access to a keyboard for all eternity. Even better, perhaps it would rain, and the defiant criminal would stay tethered to the torture seat as the winds roared and the heavens opened to drench the perpetrator with a deluge not seen since the Ark. Yes, this would earn a smile from Sister Margaret, a feat as she was known never to have smiled. Ageless, rumor had it that she had known the original Apostles and still carried a grudge that women were not allowed to join that exclusive club. She made no excuses for her dislike of men; even priests quaked in her presence, afraid of the lash of her sarcastic tongue.

"Grace."

Startled from her thoughts, Grace stuttered, "Wh-whaaat?"

"No, no, that will not do at all."

The squinting eyes were upon her as Sister bent over the top of her computer, having forced her hips between the rows. She leaned over, her breasts finding a shelf.

"Yes, Sister?" Grace tried again.

"Respect, Grace, respect. You have a beautiful name as an example for you."

"Yes, Sister."

"I'm always watching, always watching."

"Yes, Sister."

"Did you hear me say to go to the CNN website? Hurricane Katrina has hit New Orleans hard."

"Yes, Sister, I'm there."

Grace rolled her eyes at Lindsey as the tiger slipped away, sparing her for the moment, stalking new prey.

"This looks really bad," Lindsey whispered.

Grace stared at the screen as live coverage of the hurricane literally flooded it. Trees were bent over as if touching their toes in some weird work-out. Water was whooshing to six-foot levels. The Superdome was filled to the brim with thousands of people. Old ladies languished in the heat, little lost children and babies wailed. There were rumors of dead bodies floating in the flooded streets and others left behind in attics.

The heat was a major character in this drama. The freeways were still clogged with people trying to get away. The levees had broken. The city was under water.

"No doubt, ladies, we will soon begin to help in any way possible," Sister said. "We must reach out to our sister school in New Orleans."

At that moment Sister Joan, the head mistress, came on the PA and announced an immediate prayer service in the chapel.

The girls sighed together, unanimous in not wanting to spend another hour on their knees. "Ladies," Sister Margaret intoned, "let us bow our heads in a quick prayer to Saint Jude." The girls smiled, having heard often that they as lost causes should pray to Saint Jude as he apparently specialized in helping such lost souls.

Grace did as told but with head bowed, she pulled up her MySpace page and went back to final touches on her photo. If she could just get her eyes to shine more. Maybe more mascara and a different eye shadow? And maybe that wasn't the right top after all. More cleavage? Why not? She had it: everything except a boyfriend. That was her goal. Lindsey was sneaking out to see some guy from Houston High. She did a lot of bragging about how cute he was and their make-out sessions. Enhancing the photo once more, she thanked St. Jude for her ability to multi-task.

"Young ladies, to the chapel. And quiet in the halls. We have much to pray for," barked Sister Margaret.

Closing down the computer, Grace grabbed Lindsey's hand. "Almost finished," she giggled.

ESSENCE

"Get rid of those voodoo doodads," Mimmi said, her lip curled in ugliness. "Ain't no good gonna come from them. What's wrong with your mama, keeping those ugly creatures in her bedroom? No wonder we're underwater. She's tempting Satan."

"Oh, no. The devil himself?" little Chardonnai began to sob again. "He here?"

"No, of course not," Essence said, wishing Mimmi would shut up.

Essence looked around the darkened room to the table that held a collection of odd little figures. She and Chardonnai had been up in this muggy room for what seemed like days since Katrina had hit hard. The water had come on fast, drowning the yard, and still surging, sloshed into the first floor. They had stood on the couch until the water had pushed halfway up the guillotine window. Then Mimmi had hustled them up to the second floor where they now huddled in Mama's room. "Closer to heaven," she had said as they slogged to the stairs, waist deep in a gumbo of Mississippi River and Lake Pontchartrain, stirred by that old witch, Katrina. Mimmi had hoisted Chardonnai up as high as she could, giving no hint that she might have made a serious mistake in not leaving. George was the only one who seemed to be having a good time as he swam around, splashing.

Now they huddled together on the big bed, water just covering George's feet as he sniffed around the room, doubtless in search of panties. They lay on Mama's wedding quilt, hand sewn by Mimmi. Essence grabbed for a voodoo doll and pitched it out the window like a hot potato. She saw that the shed was almost drowned, only its tin roof still above water. Pieces of their life, now just debris, were treading water, unable to tell a road from a river. The little wading pool, a metal lawn chair, Mimmi's old bonnet, a plastic coke bottle, one lonely flip-flop, George's bowl, a plastic bag caught up in the treetops. An oily gumbo was seeping through the debris, making a soggy brew. Essence smacked another voodoo doll into the goop as Chardonnai cried, "Where's Mama?" she sobbed. "She can save us from the devil."

"Your mama's just fine. Probably hiding somewhere along the way. Or maybe she never left work. So she's safe there," Mimmi said. "She's probably helping other folks right now."

"Don't worry. She'll be hugging you soon," Essence added. "Look at silly old George, acting like nothing's even happened. He's not afraid of Satan." She was so mad at Mimmi she just wanted to scream at her, but knew that would really upset Char so she gritted her teeth, holding back her words.

Chardonnai stopped crying and watched George as he splashed in the water, stomping around, chasing his tail. Essence looked around her mama's room, neat in every way other than the uninvited invasion of water. Sparsely furnished with the bed, an old dresser and oaken armoire, the room's only diversion was the table of doodads. "Precious little remembrances of good times," that's what Mama called them. Beads from Mardi Gras, crayoned cards from her girls, the photo of her family.

Essence reached across Mimmi and grabbed the photo from the table. Holding it up, she touched first her mama through the glass, as always admiring her beauty. She was a tall, thin woman with beautiful curly dark hair that matched her deep brown eyes. Magical eyes to Essence. Her coffee skin, like a latte, Mimmi said, seemed to shine from the picture. Seated with her were Essence and Char. Mimmi loved telling her Essence was the image of her own mother, Grandpére's wife. Shorter and rounder than her own mama, Essence had darker skin and a big butt as Char liked to tease her, but the same magic sparkled from her eyes. She had Mama-eyes, dark as molasses jazz. Char was still an imp of a girl. She smiled from the photo, all toothy smile and corn rows. Beauty was a few years off for her.

How many times had Essence sat on this very bed and watched her mama in her best purple dress, luscious as ripe plums. She was so slim and beautiful as she looked in the mirror, putting the final bits of jewelry in her ears and rouge on her cheeks. And Mama was so smart. Hadn't she picked herself up by the boot straps, as Mimmi said, and gotten herself to school and become a nurse? A damn good one, Mimmi always bragged. Her smart and beautiful Mama would sit on the bed next to Essence, bend over, and slip her silver shoes on, and then look at Essence, smiling and say," Girl, these are Mama's dancing shoes. I work hard all week, but Saturdays are my jazz nights. Do I look delicious, girl?"

"Yes, Mama."

"And how delicious is that, girl?"

"The very essence of Mardi Gras," she would answer, finishing their game. They would collapse on the bed in a tangle of perfume and dreams, and off Mama would go into the night with some beau, as Mimmi called them. Mama said no one man was ever gonna tie her down again. No, sir, she had a good job and could put food on the table and with Mimmi's help take care of her girls. So she'd dance away the silvery night in her fancy shoes with these handsome men. But she always came back to Mimmi and her girls. Always. A tear slipped down Essence's cheek. She turned away from Chardonnai so she wouldn't see that she too wondered if they'd ever see Mama again. And they sure could use a daddy now, too, no matter what Mama said.

GRACE

"Young lady, you are in trouble now. Not even through the first week of school." Grace looked around the kitchen, fixing her eyes on the restaurant-style stove with its six gas burners. Top of the line, of course. She tried to protect her eyes from the angry onslaught of her mother. "Zero-tolerance, not just at school, but here at home."

Grace continued to examine the kitchen appliances, all hidden away cleverly behind oaken wood. Anything but direct contact with her mom's eyes would do. She was sitting at the granite island, her feet dangling from a stool while her mother paced the other side.

"How many times were you told? How many times were you forbidden to put your smug face on any computer screen? Look at me."

Grace stopped her mental tour of the kitchen knowing she'd better obey this command. She started with her mother's clinic scrubs, then let her eyes move on up to her face, to those pursed lips, then to her narrow nose, perfect, of course, and on up to her blue eyes.

"Well?"

"Does Dad know?"

"Not yet. I think you ought to tell him. Do you have any idea how embarrassing it is to be called to the school? To have to sit waiting outside Sister Joan's office, wondering what you've done now? Then to sit and listen to her explain your illegal computer crime? And then to have to look at that awful photo of you? Too much make-up. Ridiculous cleavage. Lying about your age. What is wrong with you? Why didn't you just change your name to *slut*? That's where this will all lead you. We thought you had turned a new page. Started fresh. How can I ever trust you again? Now go up to your room."

Grace saw her mother's face begin to turn violently red as she ranted on and on. Soon the tears would flow so Grace got out of the kitchen as fast as possible, making it through the dining room, into the living room, and up the stairs in record time. She would not let her mother see her cry. Bursting into her room, she ran to open the French doors that led to her balcony. Leaning over the iron rail, she gasped for breath, afraid she was going to lose her scant breakfast. Behind her she heard her mother enter the room and begin a manic tour of every outlet, unplugging every tech device in the room. Anything that ticked, talked, recorded, texted, or played would now be out of reach. "There," her mother said, very satisfied with her work, "back to the fifties for you, young lady. And I want all that make-up and the top you wore in the photo."

Grace remained out on the balcony, almost mindless of the sweat running down her face as she stood there in her blue plaid uniform and ridiculous knee socks. She preferred the Houston heat to her mother's anger.

Her mother's voice found her anyway. "You just stand out there—unplugged—and think about what you've done," she ordered, turning and leaving the room. Poor Idol stood in the doorway, afraid to come into the room, rubbing against the doorjamb as if to ask, *Have I done something wrong? Are you mad at me?*

"Come on, Idol," Grace coaxed, "Wicked Mom is gone for now." She crossed the room, stooped, and pulled the cat into her arms, hugging her tight.

Next would come one of her parents' famous cool-downs, Grace thought, realizing what a yawn her life was about to become. She had been spared expulsion and given a week's suspension, her sentence probably softened with a donation to the school from Mom. No doubt some new little alcove or statue would bear the Woodson name soon. Once Grace had grown too large for the little green time-out chair which, of course, had matched the décor of her bedroom, they had begun the cool-downs and groundings. She had spent countless hours sitting in that chair, thinking about her sins. She always seemed in a hurry to grow up and watched the wrong movies too soon, drank the wrong drinks too soon, wore her mama's make-up and jewelry too soon. Grandpa Woodson would always come and sit on her bed counting with her how long her sentence had to go. But now, Mom would get over it; she always did. Meanwhile, she'd text Lindsey who had evaded capture so far. No, she remembered she was unplugged and wireless-less. Maybe a nap. She and Idol would just curl up together for now on her soft bed.

***

She awoke to someone shaking her shoulder. She looked up into her dad's eyes. He was still dressed in one of his work suits, his paisley tie hanging in her face. His cheeks were red, too, but she knew he would be calmer than Mom. Relieved, she was sure she could get around him. For a psychiatrist, he could be pretty gullible when it came to his daughter. His eyes were not happy eyes. No loving laugh crinkles around those green eyes, also her eyes. *Here it comes*, she thought. She sat up as her dad moved away from the bed. Carrie Underwood stared from the walls at the two of them, as her dad bent over the media center, plugged in the TV, and pushed the remote.

"But..." Grace tried.

He stood there as Wolf Blitzer reporting from CNN filled the screen, then faded, voicing over image after image of the people of New Orleans. Katrina had done her work. The coverage focused on the people stranded at the Superdome. Buses had finally been sent to begin to transport them to the Astrodome in Houston. It seemed that Katrina was now in Grace's backyard, floating debris in her wake right into their lives. She had made invisible landfall in Houston.

"Look at this, Grace. Look," her father ordered, turning back to her. "You have far too much in life. You abuse everything you have and everyone who loves you. Look at these people who have lost everything."

The images continued to fill the screen, on old woman dangling from a helicopter, dogs howling on small islands in flooded streets, a black girl her age holding her younger sister as they huddled in a small wooden boat.

"These people have been evacuated to the Superdome. Thousands are cramped there in filthy conditions just hoping for a drink of water. Now some of them are going to be sent here to the Astrodome. I'll be there to help," her dad continued.

Super Doctor Dad to the rescue, Grace thought. *Spare me.*

"And you, my darling daughter, since your disobedience has earned you a week off from school, you will be going with me to help."

"But..."

"Don't say a word to me. Just say to yourself, 'MySpace is now the Astrodome.'"

"Whatever," sighed Grace, disgusted with life in general.

ESSENCE

Essence and Chardonnai huddled together in seats in the semi-darkness of the arena. It was beyond hot. They could see up to a huge hole in the dome ceiling blown off by Katrina. *What a funny name for a storm*, Essence had thought, imagining a big lady with cheeks puffed full, huffing and puffing the roof half off the place. *Nothing super about this dome to that old gal, Katrina.* Chardonnai began to cry again, asking for Mimmi and Mama, even George. They were alone now, and Essence knew it was up to her to protect and comfort her little sister.

"Little girl. Honey? You two all alone here?"

Essence looked up to see a lady about the age and size of Mimmi leaning over them. "Why, I'd sit a spell with you two, but I'd bust through this flimsy seat in no time. I just sent Harold to get some water for us. And for you, too."

Essence's ears picked up at the familiar name. Harold. Could it be? Remembering her manners as Mimmi would want her to, she introduced herself and Char to the kind lady.

"Now, child, I'm Mrs. Beaudrie, and I'm very pleased to meet you and your sister, Char. You tell me the story of how you got here all alone," she said, plopping right down on the aisle and pulling Chardonnai onto her lap. "And what's this beautiful quilt you have so tight 'round your shoulders?"

***

"Anybody up there?" a man had called above the low putter of the motor on his boat.

Essence had turned to Mimmi, her eyes questioning, her mouth afraid to answer. Her grandma had moved off the bed fast, grabbed a pillow, and yanked the case off it. Damp as it was, it worked as she leaned out the window, waving it in a call for help. The water was up to her ankles in Mimmi's bedroom, but had stopped rising.

"Here, here," she yelled. "Help us."

"How many?" the man shouted, idling the motor.

"Who are you?" Mimmi asked. She looked down into an old aluminum boat, carrying two men, both dressed in old, rough jeans and plaid shirts, their boots covered with a small lake of dirty water in the bottom of the boat.

Essence moved from the bed, pushing her aside. This was no time for old politeness and introductions. He wasn't one of her mama's beaus come to call. They wouldn't be here if not for this old woman's refusal to leave. Chardonnai rose up from the bed, fear in her eyes.

"I'm Josh, ma'am. And this here's Ben."

"Well, young man, I am pleased to meet you," answered Mimmi, giving Essence a shove with her hip as she strained to look over the peeling windowsill to see their rescuers. She looked down on him, sitting in the back of the small aluminum boat, his hand on the motor behind him, peering up at her through his sunglasses. "Let me see your eyes, Josh."

Essence couldn't believe this, but she was wedged back from the window, unable to move forward.

"Yes, ma'am," Josh said, pulling his glasses off with his left hand, still idling the motor with his right hand.

"Well, I do see truth in those eyes," Mimmi called down,

"So I'll tell you there are three of us up here. Me and my granddaughters, Essence and Chardonnai. Girls, say hello to this young man who's come to rescue us."

She moved back just enough to let the two girls lean out under her watchful eye. "Good morning, sir," little Chardonnai shouted, trying to project her voice over the motor's rattle. "And you, too, sir," she said nodding at Ben.

"Now, Essence," Mimmi prodded.

"Please, kind sir, get us the hell out of here," Essence called down.

If it hadn't been for the men's hearty laughs, Essence knew she would have received one of Mimmi's smacks across her bottom. No time for that now. No time to enforce the no-cursing truth. Besides, George took that moment to make himself known by pushing up to the window and barking, his tongue hanging out over the sill from his silly French head.

"Ma'am, we've got room for you and the girls, but not the dog," Ben called up from the front of the boat.

"Oh, no," Mimmi called back. "We can't leave George. He's my only grandson."

"Sorry, ma'am. Orders. Pets have to stay. They'll be rescued later."

Josh had maneuvered closer, and the boat now sat beneath the window next to the shed.

"Have you got something to stand on?" Ben yelled as Josh cut the motor.

"Yes," Essence called back as she pulled the small table over, sweeping Mama's memories onto the bed. She and Mimmi had the same thought at the same time.

"That's a mighty puny table for my hefty behind," Mimmi said, rolling her eyes. "You girls better go first."

"We're not leaving you," Essence cried.

"Now, girls, I didn't say that at all."

Essence knew that Mimmi needed pills for her diabetes. She knew there were only a few left in the small red bottle on the dresser. She would die if she didn't get out of this house soon. She pulled Chardonnai over the table, hoisted her up, and called out to Josh below. "Here's our Chardonnai." Poor little Chardonnai closed her eyes tight, afraid to look below.

"Okay, Char," Josh called up to her, "Just walk out onto the top of the shed."

"I can't watch," Mimmi said. "You do it, Essence." She plopped back down on the bed with a sigh.

Essence had her arms around Char, leaned to kiss her on top of the head, and gave her a little push, then watched helpless as her little sister stood alone. The shed was holding her weight so far. Josh stood up in the boat, and it began to rock. Reaching out, he grabbed the tiny girl, turned fast, and handed her over to Ben. Not wasting a moment, Ben plopped her on the aluminum seat. Not until then did she begin to cry softly.

"Hush, now, Char, honey. You're safe," Mimmi called from above. "Go, Essence. Char needs you in that rickety boat."

"Promise you'll follow me," she said, looking down into the brown eyes she loved best in the world, even more than Mama's.

"Course I will. You think I'd leave my best gals alone?" She patted Essence on the behind, and gave her a big smooch on her lips. "Hmmm, love that sugar," she said, a line they'd used to say goodnight forever. "Now, Essence, you take your mama's wedding quilt with you to keep you safe. Best thing your mama got from her marriage besides you and Chardonnai." Leaning out the window, Mimmi tossed the quilt down into the boat and Josh grabbed it.

Assured, Essence then put one knee up onto the table, hoping it would hold, and out the window she went, crouching tentatively on the shed. She had no chance to even look around before Josh stood again and pulled her down by the waist into the boat. Char grabbed for her, and the two sat on the aluminum seat together, arm in arm, shivering in fear.

Above them, for a minute they saw Mimmi's face in the window. Then there was a crash and a splintering of wood and she disappeared. Silence. Chardonnai began to wail and Essence hugged her harder and called out, "Mimmi?"

Mimmi stuck her head out the window and called to Josh, "I'm okay. That flimsy table was no match for my butt. You take my girls and leave me here for now with George. Get my girls to the Dome, you hear?"

"You promised, Mimmi! You promised," Essence sobbed. "You've never lied to me."

"Well, here's a truth for you. Sometimes lying is the only way. Just white lies. And that table made the final decision. Now go, Josh. Take care of those babies."

"Yes, ma'am," Josh called, wrapping the quilt around the girls.

Essence rose up in the boat, wanting with all her heart to return to the bedroom in the old white house, but Josh pushed her down. He sat back down on the seat, trying hard to settle the boat in its rocking, and tugged at the pull-start. Essence pulled Char tight to her under the quilt and tapped the photo in her pocket for luck. "Daddy," she whispered, "please help us."

From above, the girls heard Mimmi crooning. She was singing about that lazy river again. The girls cried.

GRACE

Grace lay beside the pool, her hand skimming the warm water. It was another lazy August afternoon. She sat up and reached for the tall glass of lemonade Lindsey carried from the kitchen. Linda, their cook, made the best lemonade. It slid down your throat in a perfect blend of sweet and sour, the crushed ice its own a/c.

"You know what would make this even better? More refreshing?" Lindsey asked, handing the drink over to Grace.

"Don't even think of my dad's vodka," Grace snapped. "I'm in enough trouble."

"Chill, Gracie," Lindsey said, plopping down on a deck chair. "You poor little girl, suffering in this awful prison."

Grace looked around her. The patio and deck were just right, in impeccable taste. The smell of chlorine rose from the welcoming pool. She could close her eyes and remember Troy, the decorator, leaning over the plans for the pool area. Talking to her mom in a breathless voice, he had pointed out a proposed rock garden which would climb up from the pool, a stand of birches behind it assuring privacy. The slope would be planted with vines of Star Jasmine and Trailing Lantana curling among the rocks. Near the rock garden would be the bar and table, protected by a large striped umbrella and backed by a hedge of Texas sage. Swinging around the oval pool from the eating area would be the lounging area, decked with red, white, and blue chairs and couches. To the left of the French doors would be tubs of graceful Spanish Dagger, their large stalks in creamy white bloom. Rounding the other end of the pool, guests would have access to a small pool house, Jacuzzi, and shower. Again providing privacy, a hedge of fragrant Primrose Jasmine would stand guard. Of course, her mom had been sold on the plans, and sparing no cost, the pool area had been christened within a few months in time for the summer season. Absolute perfection. And Grace had increased her knowledge of Houston plants and trees again, digging with her shovel and patting with her hands.

Older, she and Lindsey had often perched on the bar stools, sneaking vodka into their drinks. Once they had even managed to make a pitcher of Long Island Ice Tea. Barely able to walk after that experiment, they'd needed a long siesta after collapsing into the deck chairs. What a sunburn they'd had later, their bodies as red as the chairs. That touch of "flu" had gone away in days under her mom's unsuspecting care.

"Grace."

She snapped back to attention as her dad appeared. Stepping through the French doors onto the patio, he held his hand to his eyes to avoid the sun. At his feet Grace saw her cat poking her way out the door.

"Dad," she cried, jumping up, "Idol's trying to get out."

Her dad bent down and scooped Idol into his arms. "Got her," he said. "I just wanted to warn you girls not to stay out here too long. You don't want to fry."

"Don't worry," Grace said. She knew her dad was "working from home" to keep an eye on her. Some of his patients came for their appointments here. He saw them in his den, and even though there was a separate entrance directly to his office, she sometimes saw the stray boy or girl. She was always curious to know more. Doctor Dad was always close-mouthed about his little "loonies" as she called them. Once she'd thought she'd recognized a boy from school, but knew better than to ask. It amazed her they'd never taken her to a shrink. Probably thought they could give her a home cure if she got too nuts.

Carrying little Idol, her dad made himself scarce again. Grace supposed they were okay about her suspension to let Lindsey come over after school. She had brought her homework—more boring French verbs and an essay assignment for *To Kill a Mockingbird*. Aha, she thought. They'd have to let her use her computer to write that.

"Too bad you missed school today," said Lindsey, laughing.

The two girls were sitting on deck chairs opposite each other. Lindsey leaned over towards Grace and said, "You know how Jack has been kinda showing up around me?"

"Yeah," Grace replied, looking at Lindsey through her dark shades. She really was attractive. They both watched the junk food so they looked good in their bikinis. Too bad she'd included that photo on her page, too. That had been the final straw for old Sister Margaret. They had laughed, imagining the old nun's bulging eyes and that thumping vein on her forehead as she pounced on that photo. Lindsey had that unusual combination of blue eyes and red hair. Grace called her her personal "I Love Lucy girl." So, no, Grace wasn't surprised that Jack was hanging around, but she was a bit surprised that Lindsey was interested as she'd been sneaking around with the guy from Houston High. Jack attended the St. Catherine's Middle School for Boys that had opened only a few years ago, housed on the third floor of their building. The elementary school was co-ed, but the sexes were separated from fifth through eighth grades. Of course, her parents had read research that said such a separation improved concentration on one's studies. The nuns were ever-vigilant of any contact between the sexes. They shared no classes. No recess, no lunch. Like poor Romeo and Juliet, they could only hope for a brief glimpse in the chapel during the liturgies. But it hadn't taken the boys long to discover that if they stood by the windows of their history class on the third floor, they could look down and zero in on the ladies in their art class on the first floor as the wing curved around surrounding the courtyard. They didn't dare make the trip down the flights of stairs to the girls' rooms so they worshipped from above.

But today Jack had dared.

"So," Lindsey said, leaning over to get close to Grace, insuring her voice didn't carry across the pool, "the guys got to school and there was Jack with a dozen roses for, guess who?"

"Really?" Grace said. Giggling, she pulled her sunglasses down to the end of her nose. "Do tell all, girl."

"I was a little late getting here because I ran into Bob when I got home," Lindsey continued. Bob was Jack's best friend and Lindsey's neighbor. He had filled Lindsey in on the details.

"And..." Grace wanted Lindsey to spill all the dirt fast.

"So he said Jack was standing in the back of Ms. Meyer's classroom, trying to hide the roses from her. She's not dumb so she spotted him and walked back to where Bob was standing. So Bob told her about the roses and said what Jack's plan was."

"What'd she say?" Grace asked, putting her empty glass down on the table between them.

"She's always laughing at the way the guys look down at us from the window, kinda like a reverse Romeo and Juliet balcony scene."

"With way too many actors," laughed Grace.

"Well, she went back to Jack and asked him who the flowers were for. He told her and asked if she thought it would be possible to run the blockade and get past Sister Margaret. Ms. Meyer's favorite saying is, 'It's easier to beg forgiveness than ask permission,' so she was prepared to look the other way. But when about six of the guys headed for the stairway, she stopped them, explaining that that big a contingency just might draw fire from Sister Margaret's artillery. Maybe two guys could stay under her radar."

Grace reached for the sunscreen for even though they had dark August tans and were in the shade, the Texas sun could still do harm. "Turn around," she said, "I'll get your back."

NOLA Gals/Barbara J. Rebbeck

Lindsey half-turned so she could still see Grace's face as she talked on. "So I'm by my locker and unaware of all this, just lost in the usual clanging of metal doors and shouting, everyone rushing not to be late for morning assembly. Madison runs up to me, all red-faced and irritating. She stands there and goes, 'Lindsey, Jack and Bob are down by the stairwell,' in that annoying voice. So I look down the hall and see first Jack and then Bob coming into the hallway. Then I spot the red roses. And behind them, gaining speed is Sister Margaret."

"Oh, no," Grace laughed in mock-horror as Lindsey rose from the chair and moved behind her to demonstrate what happened next.

"I watch as she swoops over Jack's shoulder, crushes him against her chest, and grabs the sinful roses," she said, repeating the actions with Grace as the prey.

"I can't breathe," Grace shouted.

Releasing Grace and sitting back down, Lindsey continued, "So Sister Margaret shouts, 'Roses for me? How thoughtful.' Then she lets go of Jack and points to the stairs with a grand sweep of her arm. But Jack manages to shout that the roses are for me before he and Jack disappear back up the stairs."

Grace laughed out loud, wishing she'd been there for this little play. "Were you in trouble? Then what?"

"I turn around, hoping I can crawl into my locker. My face must be bright red. Madison is still there. You know she soooo hopes I'm in big trouble. 'Lindsey,' I hear and I know it's got to be Sister Margaret herself. She stares down at me, her hand raised above her head, clutching only the most beautiful red roses you've ever seen. I'm sure she's gonna bash me over the head with them, thorns and all."

"What did she say?"

"'Lindsey,' she says, lowering the flowers, 'I believe these are for you. I shall put them in water, and you may have them at the end of the day.'"

"No," Grace said.

"Oh, yes, so you can imagine how surprised Bob was to see me coming up my driveway with the roses after school. Bob said their language arts teacher gave them a lesson on writing love poems for young ladies this afternoon," Lindsey laughed.

Grace giggled, knowing it would not be long before Lindsey would be reading her a poem from Jack.

ESSENCE

"This place is so scary," Char whispered, her face pressed into her sister's chest, her hands clutching Mama's quilt around her shoulders.

"Tell me the story of that old quilt," Essence said, trying to cheer Char up.

"No, you tell it," Char said, spreading the quilt out in her arms.

"Well, Mimmi sewed that quilt for weeks for a surprise for Mama and old Harold's wedding. Each patch shows something about our family story. Like this one that shows the old coal barge coming down the Mississippi. Who knew that barge would turn into our old white house? And this one shows that shiny trumpet of Daddy's."

"With molasses music drops," Char added, cuddling closer, but still holding out the quilt. "And what about this one?" she pointed.

"Why, you know that one. It shows Mimmi and Pippi on

their wedding day many years ago. And there's Mama as a tiny baby," she said, pointing to another square.

"Where's the gumbo one?" Char asked, searching.

"Right here, silly, it's the old family recipe," Essence pointed, tiring of this game. "So what do you think this old dome looks like?" she asked, tucking the quilt back around Char.

"A big, scary, messy, hot place. I'm so hot," Char replied.

"Then take off the quilt," Essence said, tugging at it.

"No," Char said, "Got to keep it close." She twisted herself away from Essence, sitting up straight, leaning forward, her little brown eyes searching the semi-dark arena like a cornered animal. "I want Mama. I want Mimmi. I want George," she shouted, rocking back and forth in the uncomfortable stadium seat. They were in Row G of the section where they'd hurried when the wind had lifted a chunk of the roof off in a deafening roar.

"You know," Essence tried again, "this place reminds me of an animal. I just can't think which one. Can you, Char?"

"It's like we're inside. Like some huge animal ate us for dinner," Char said, distracted for a moment.

"Well, what animal?"

"I know. A big old snapping turtle," Char said. "Yes, ma'am, we're inside some big turtle."

"And what's its name?" asked Essence, continuing the game.

"Satchmo," giggled Char, dropping the quilt behind her on the seat as she stood up, pointing her thin little arms to the ceiling. "We're inside Satchmo's shell. He ate us in one big swallow."

"Well, I guess he just crawled up a lazy river and was so hungry he gobbled all these people down," Essence laughed, sweeping her arm around the arena. She knew at once that was the wrong thing to say as she watched Char's face crumple like a marshmallow being roasted too hot.

"Mimmi," Char mumbled, sitting back down. "She was singing that song."

"Why don't you try to sleep?" Essence said.

They'd both had little sleep all night, restless and afraid. Mrs. Beaudrie, their new friend, had sat with them, at times dozing off and once snoring as loud as Katrina. She was guarding a case for

NOLA Gals/Barbara J. Rebbeck

Harold, as she called the mysterious man the girls had yet to see. He'd returned, she'd said, while the girls were sleeping and had gone off again, leaving one bottle of water behind for them to share. Mrs. Beaudrie had pulled some crackers and two sticky candy bars from her big pockets on her flowered skirt and let them share the sweet-tasting meal. She was very talkative and had drawn a crowd around her. She was one of those people whose heart was big enough to fill the dome, and one by one she had made herself mama to a parade of New Orleans folks here in Row G. But now her new big family had overflowed into Rows F and H. Mrs. Beaudrie sat, her eyes darting back and forth, up and down, guarding her new brood as she sat in the aisle, a Cajun pied piper.

"I wish I could feed you all a spicy jambalaya, *mes chers*," she shouted, "but don't you worry. I've heard the buses are coming soon to get us all out of here. Let's all close our eyes and thank the Lord we made it through the night. He'll get us on the road soon and right on out of this old snapping turtle," she laughed, reaching over to poke Char in the side. "Oh, Lord," she said, "lead us to the light."

The sun was trickling through the gap in the roof, revealing from aisle to aisle, from row to row, from section to section the thousands of stranded people of New Orleans. The floor of the arena was a soggy carpet. Hundreds of empty water bottles, drenched blankets, the odd lawn chair, gray plastic bins, ketchup-stained paper plates, black plastic trash bags, bulging suitcases, rickety cots, even a few shopping carts covered the floor, all abandoned when the water had poured through the rafters, sending people scurrying for higher ground. The light skipped over the trash like a police searchlight, revealing mounds of rotting flotsam. Even worse than the sight of the debris was its stench.

"It stinks," Char whispered to Essence, knowing Mimmi would tell her that was not a polite word. She needed to go to the bathroom really bad, but was holding it in, afraid.

"I know," Essence said, "But we'll be gone soon."

"Where are we going?" asked Char, her brows raised.

"Mrs. Beaudrie, where are we going?" Essence asked.

"Not sure. Folks are saying Texas."

Just then a tall, thin man came bounding up the stairs. As he made it to Row G, he stopped, spotted Mrs. Beaudrie and her expanded family and announced, "Everyone, Mrs. Beaudrie, we are all going to Houston, Texas. Yippee Kiyee! Yes, sir. Houston, Texas to the Astrodome.

"Another damn dome?" Mrs. Beaudrie said, her eyes popping in dismay.

Char sucked in her breath, knowing Mimmi would not approve of such language.

"Where you been, Old Man?" she continued. "Thought you had abandoned me."

"And your new dozens of kin?" he laughed, gesturing around him. "Pass me that case if you don't mind."

The girls leaned forward, hoping there might be water, or even better, more sweets in the precious case Mrs. Beaudrie had guarded all night. She leaned over and pulled it out from under her billowy skirt with the big pockets where it had hid all night.

"Girls, this here is Harold's precious baby," she said, her eyes twinkling as she passed the case to Harold.

A shadow came over the rip in the roof as Harold leaned over, blocking the sun, his green eyes flashing, his lips breaking into a huge smile which revealed white, white teeth as pearly as Old Satchmo's. Essence touched the photo tucked in her pocket. The sun resumed its search on the arena, shooting a halo around old Harold as he leaned over and said directly to Essence, "Sweet Gal, I'm going to play you a tune sweet as molasses." It was as if the photo had caught on fire, feeding a hot flush of certainty right to her heart. She knew without a doubt that this man was her daddy. And she knew for sure what he hid in that case.

"So Harold, will we ever see the Seventh Ward again?" asked Mrs. Beaudrie.

"You bet, ma'am. We'll be back. The Big Easy will rise again. Now let me play your new kin a tune. Something sweet."

"Of course," Essence said, her heart bursting with love. Chardonnai smiled, too, looking up at the strange man with hope for the first time in days.

NOLA Gals/Barbara J. Rebbeck

He carefully placed the case in the aisle one row down from Char's seat, bent down, and flipped the catches to unlock it. Char leaned over, unknowing, excited. Harold pulled the top up to reveal a shiny trumpet.

"Look," Char shouted, "it's just like the one on Mama's quilt."

Picking up the horn, he stood and put it to his lips. He began to play a tune, soft at first, then louder. A hush fell over Mrs. Beaudrie's chattering kin as the notes floated above the hot debris of the dome. Essence closed her eyes, and Char giggled as the tune spread from row to row, then section to section, its jazzy message of hope rising. Essence dared not look, for she knew by heart from her dream what this man—her father—looked like as he played. He stood, his trumpet to his lips, cheeks puffed, and bending back, his knees bent, and his feet apart. Eyes closed, his fingers pressed the taps in a magic dance, squeezing out the music, melting the molasses.

"The river," Char whispered and began to sing along. Essence froze, unable to sing, adrift in a bitter sweetness.

GRACE WOODSON
Skin Deep
Essay, September 4, 2005

I grew up today. I had slogged through the required summer reading of To Kill a Mockingbird, prodded by my mom and dad who kept assuring me it was a great book, that Harper Lee had won the Pulitzer Prize for it. As the summer wore on, I had said I would read a synopsis of it online, not to worry. That had caused a small explosion on my mom's part, and a directive to sit in front of her and REALLY read the book, out loud if necessary. So for several nights we sat together as I grew to know the residents of Maycomb through little Scout's eyes, walking in her shoes or sometimes, bare feet. But today, I really did crawl into the skins of others, and now I think I understand what a very wise attorney named Atticus Finch was trying to teach his children, Scout and Jem in 1932 in Maycomb, Alabama. What he meant when he told them:

> "First of all," he said, "if you can learn a simple trick, Scout, you'll get along a lot better with all kinds of folks. You never really understand a person until you consider things from his point of view—"

OLA Gals/Barbara J. Rebbeck

"Sir?"

"—until you climb into his skin and walk around in it."

(Lee, 33)

Everyone knows I am at home for a few days, having been a bad girl, having violated the ban against having a MySpace page. But what you may not know is how I have been spending my time. Poolside? No. Singing along with Carrie Underwood? No. Blogging and text messaging? No. Much like Scout Finch, I have been beside my dad and learning life lessons. I have a new appreciation for everyone and everything in my own life as I have been inside the skins of people, "refugees" as some call them who have nothing, and in some cases, no one. I have been with my dad, a psychiatrist, at the Astrodome, helping him help the survivors of Katrina. I have seen firsthand what Atticus meant when he said..."there were other ways of making people into ghosts." (12)

I was, of course, very nervous after my dad had informed me that I would be spending time with him at the Astrodome. I knew better than to argue with him. I'm not that dumb. So Thursday as we left, my usual chatty personality had been broken like one of the levees in New Orleans. I had been allowed to break the technology ban I'd been under since my MySpace sin to see coverage of the wreck the city now was. I had seen on CNN shots of people being helicoptered out of flooded neighborhoods. I had seen footage of movie stars trying to rescue children. Forlorn pets, left behind, stood abandoned on old cars which had become islands in the murky water. What could I possibly do to help these strangers?

My dad had been at the Astrodome the day before, returning exhausted late at night. The first buses of evacuees had arrived early in the morning. Thousands filled the arena. Now as we pulled into the huge parking lot, I clutched my copy of *Mockingbird* and my journal. Maybe I could hide somewhere and read.

We parked the car in the special Volunteer Section and started into the stadium. It was hot and muggy. I looked straight ahead, aware that my dad had slipped his arm around my shoulder. "Ready?" he asked. "You'll be fine, Grace. Just be yourself."

I was not prepared for what I saw as we entered the huge arena. Thousands of people. Some sitting, some lying on cots. Some roaming. Some talking. We passed a section where the walls were covered with notes and photos of the missing. Many stood, reading, crying, and some posting new additions to the boards. Immediately, I was Scout, in the novel, standing on the street in front of the mysterious Boo Radley's house. I was scared. I was in these poor folks' skin. Here I stood gazing out at thousands of survivors from a cruel storm, wanting to cry with them. In fact, tears did start to crawl down my cheeks. My dad leaned over and hugged me, and I asked him what I could possibly do. He said to go pick up some water bottles and pointed over to a small group of kids sitting on cots a few feet away. "Just offer them the water and see if they want to talk."

So I did as he suggested, and with the water, approached the little group. Sitting there were a girl about my age and what must have been her younger sister, wrapped in a quilt, in spite of the heat. As I came near, two little boys came and sat with them. A large woman seemed to protect them like a big umbrella. Beside her sat a thin man, clutching of all things, a trumpet. I screwed up all my courage, smiled, and asked if they'd like some water. "Why, thank you, young lady," the umbrella-mama said. "Are you that nice doctor's daughter?" She went on to explain that he had talked to them yesterday and made them feel right at home. I sat down, lost for words, but hoping to try.

I found the two girls and boys, almost frantic with horrible stories of being trapped and then rescued, only to sit in the stench of the Superdome before being bused to Houston.

Essence, as the older girl called herself, seemed still a bit in shock, repeating over and over how their dog, George and grandmother, Mimmi were still missing. The youngest, Chardonnai kept asking for her mom. "What's that book you got?" asked the old man. I explained the reading assignment and a little bit about the book. How Scout tells the story of her dad's bravery in

NOLA Gals/Barbara J. Rebbeck

defending a black man against false charges. The woman, Mrs. Beaudrie and the man with the trumpet both said they had heard of it, but never read it themselves. "Read us some," they all said. Glad to have something to do, I opened the book and began to read. I had to really speak up and was glad for Mrs. Hart's speech classes which I'd always hated as I began to really act out the book for the tiny group. As I read though, I noticed out of the corner of my eye, more people gathering, sitting, staring at me as I unfolded the story of Scout and her father's small southern town.

Along about the time I got to the part where Atticus tells Scout you can make a person a ghost mostly by ignoring them, Essence suddenly broke through my little play-acting, shouting, "That's what they done to us. We're just thousands of ghosts who've been nearly drowned, baked in the dome, roasted in long bus lines, and plopped here. Boo! We're haunting you forever," she cried, rising and swooping her arms out before her. I'd have laughed, but tears were rolling down her cheeks. I looked at her in her dirty shirt, raggedy jeans, flip flops, and knew I was lucky to be in my own skin.

At that point, the skinny man who still had not said his name, began to play a slow, sad tune on his trumpet. From another cot, a man and woman began to sing along about missing New Orleans, their eyes closed, as if they were freed from this arena, flying with the mockingbirds home.

"Let's have us a parade for all the ghosts," Chardonnai said as they all rose and formed a line. "Come on, Grace," she said, grabbing my hand.

"Not ghosts. How about saints?" said Mrs. Beaudrie. "Old Man, you know that one. Play us a tune."

And so we formed a rag-tag parade of New Orleans ghosts, weaving up and down the rows of cots, picking up recruits as we marched, singing about the saints marching in. Yes, I was in their skins and honored to be there. We had nothing but the clothes on our backs, some water, and cool jazz. As we swayed back and forth, I thought I saw Scout and her older brother, Jem from the book way up in the balcony, peering down at us, and over by the missing person wall, I was sure I saw Atticus, the wise lawyer and my dad, planning how to help everyone, how to bring these ghosts back to life.

ESSENCE
Journal
September 3, 2005

That nice girl Grace gave me this journal and a pen to write with. She said it might make me feel better to write down all my thoughts about all that's happened. So I will try. I'm not good at writing. My teachers always told me so. I will try writing for Grace. Maybe she will be my friend. I miss my friends mostly little Billy. I hope he is safe. With Mama, Mimmi and old George somewhere.

Here is what happened to me and my family.

We had waited a long time in the hot sun at the Superdome. Surely hell must be cooler. We were always looking for Mimmi and Mama. Where were they? Would I ever see them again? And where was that skinny old George? Hours and hours in line while the buses lined up and filled up one by one. Little Chardonnai finally peed her pants, but that was okay. We were going to go to Texas. Houston they said. All around us was trash that was stinking and rotting, and some people on the ground too old or weak to stand up just like the trash. It was the worst smell I had ever smelled. Dead bodies, Mrs. Beaudrie said. She was a nice old lady who had taken us to her bosom as she said. The man with the trumpet never said much. Maybe he was my daddy, but if he was, he sure didn't want to know it so I kept my silly mouth shut. I could hear Mimmi telling me a truth that trouble would be just around the corner if I let him know what I guessed about him. I felt I would melt like a popsicle if we didn't get on that bus soon. Slowly we moved closer. Folks said the buses had air. That would be worth the wait. Then there were people yelling and gunshots. Chardonnai and I sat hard on the ground behind Mrs. Beaudrie. Scared as hell. Sorry to talk that way. Then a soldier came by with a gun and told us to stand up cuz our bus was next. Finally finally finally. First Harold hopped up the stairs. I only called him his name in my head so as not to scare him off. Next he reached down for Chardonnai. She went up the stairs with me behind her. Last

NOLA Gals/Barbara J. Rebbeck

came Mrs. Beaudrie, squeezing her big behind through the narrow aisle. Chardonnai and I sat next to each other and watched the rest of the bus fill up. Mrs. Beaudrie and the trumpet man sat in front of us. When it was packed solid, the driver stood and welcomed us all. Everybody cheered. The door closed, and the air came on. Hallelujah! shouted Mrs. Beaudrie. We are leaving from the gates of hell. That's the last I remembered as the cool of the air blew cross my face and Chardonnai with only a little smell of pee curled up beside me.

I dreamed while I was asleep on the bus. In my dream Mama and Mimmi were walking along the river with George on a leash. He was jerking along like he was trying to get away. He looked all around maybe hoping Billy would throw that old yellow ball for him to chase after. I yelled at them to wait up for me. Mama turned and said, Essence, little gal, you can't walk with us anymore. Here, take George. With that George came leaping at me covering me with his wet dog-smelly kisses pushing me down to my knees and slobbering all over me. When I looked past him, Mama and Mimmi were gone. Just gone.

GRACE

An excellent essay. You have really connected with Scout and Atticus. You have taken your suspension and with the help of your parents, used it as a time of personal growth in the face of one of the greatest tragedies in our nation's history. Will you stay in touch with Essence? I hope you are keeping a journal of your experiences. Grade- A+

Grace was pleased with the grade she'd received on her essay. She'd e-mailed back to Ms. Rodgers in record time. She knew Ms. Rodgers would understand her take on it all. And yes, she was keeping a journal. She'd had to buy a new one when she had given hers to Essence. She had returned to the Dome on Saturday and read much more of *Mockingbird* to her little class.

NOLA Gals/Barbara J. Rebbeck

They had loved it and laughed and cried at Scout's adventures, admiring her daddy's courage in defending a black man of raping a white girl. They had listened intently as she read about the mysterious neighbor, Boo Radley, who never left his house. Then she had helped Essence and Chardonnai write a description for their missing mom and grandmother, letting them use her phone number as a contact:

> PLEASE HELP FIND Mimmi LaFontaine,
> The sweetest grandmama ever.
> She has a big heart and a big butt
> With gray curly hair cut short
> And dark brown eyes and big feet.
> She is diabetic and needs her pills
> in the red bottle.
> Bless you for helping.

Their second note read:

> PLEASE HELP FIND Mama LaFontaine,
> The best mom ever.
> She is beautiful with latte skin.
> She is a nurse who helps people.
> Bless you for helping.

And their final note:

> PLEASE HELP FIND George, our dog.
> He is a white French poodle, big
> and skinny.
> He loves to eat nasty dainties.
> But we want him back anyway.
> Bless you for helping.

Watching them tack the notes on the wall had brought her to tears as she tried to imagine what it would be like if these were her missing parents. Little Chardonnai had insisted on drawing pictures of both her mama and Mimmi on the notes, although anyone would be hard put to identify them from the childish sketches. She had drawn her mom in her purple party dress with her special gold earrings. And she drew Mimmi on the porch of her beloved shotgun house, waiting to chat with the neighbor lady on the old swing, a jug of sweet tea on the little wicker table, sweating in the shade, circled by little pink flowered glasses, waiting for company.

Finally, when she had left for the day, Grace had given the novel to Essence to finish. Secretly, Grace wondered what Harper Lee would think of all this. She knew that the author was still alive, but very reclusive, almost like her character, Boo Radley. Maybe she would have joined the impromptu parade of southern ghosts at the Astrodome. Maybe she would have seen thousands of innocent mockingbirds perched in the arena, their brave songs piercing the humid semi-darkness.

"Grace?" her mom's voice interrupted her attempt at ESP with Harper Lee. "Can you come down? I need to talk to you."

"Okay," she yelled back. She'd been getting along much better with her parents since watching her dad work at the Dome. She'd been very proud as she watched him with so many kids, talking and soothing their fears. She turned down her music, Carrie of course, and hurried down the stairs wondering what was up.

Her mom was leaning against the sink, munching on a carrot stick. On the counter she'd laid out a healthy selection of veggies and salsa and a pitcher of icy lemonade. Grace sat down and made herself a plate of snacks. *Start with the positive*, she thought. "I just got an e-mail from Ms. Rodgers. She loved my essay and said I really understood Atticus."

Her mom poured her a glass of lemonade, saying, "Good for you. What grade did you get?"

"An A-plus with no revision needed," Grace replied with a certain amount of pride.

"That's my girl. Back on track."

"You know," Grace continued, pausing only for a drink of juice, "I've been thinking about Dad a lot. Do you think he's like Atticus? I mean he sure showed courage at the Dome. He just jumped in and started helping. He seemed to be so kind. He knew exactly what to do to comfort those poor people."

"That's called empathy, my dear. Do we get to read your essay now?"

"Maybe. So Dad is pretty smart, huh? Don't get me wrong, I don't mean that you're dumb or anything, but..."

"Of course he's intelligent. You don't get to be a psychiatrist without all the traits you're talking about, Grace."

"I've always thought you were cool, too. You're so good with little dogs and kitties."

"Goodness, my daughter just may have grown into her name. Grace, at last. May I give you a hug?" She rounded the counter and leaned over and gave Grace a big bear hug, but not before Grace saw tears in her eyes.

"What's up?" They looked up to see Dad coming through the patio doorway, home from work. He walked over and joined the hug, then grabbed for a carrot.

Her parents were standing in the kitchen, leaning against the sink, munching on carrot and celery sticks. They were all in a good mood. Whatever was coming, they were the picture of a united front. Grace said, "So what's up?"

"Well, Gracie, your dad called me earlier about this."

"About what?" Grace searched her mind but could think of nothing bad she'd done. No new sins in her book.

Mom said, "You know the Red Cross is working to place all the people from New Orleans in temporary homes."

"Yeah?"

"Well, your dad and I would like to know how you would feel about having Essence and Chardonnai come to live here with us for a while," her mom said, looking Grace directly in the eyes.

"Mrs. Beaudrie and Harold have taken an apartment temporarily, but feel they need our help with the two girls. They'll be getting government assistance soon," her dad continued.

Here was the test, Grace realized. Courage? Empathy? She squirmed around on the stool, realizing how this act of kindness would really change her life.

"Would they go to St. Catherine's?"

"Yes, that's fine with all the staff there. Apparently, St. Cat's will be taking in about ten girls and five boys," her mom said.

"So?" her dad asked.

"How could I look my children in the face..." Grace began

to quote Atticus Finch when he knew he had to be a model of tolerance for his kids by taking the case and defending a black man in a very white court system. Not an easy task, but one he had to do to live with himself.

Her mom leaped over and jumped on her, hugging her. "That's our Gracie. Our mature Grace."

"And she's quoting Atticus Finch, not Carrie Underwood," laughed her dad.

Just to assure her she was still an immature kid, she added, "Did you hear *American Idol* is dedicating one of their tour concerts next week to Katrina survivors? I wonder if Essence likes to listen to Carrie."

"You can certainly teach her all she'll ever want to know about her," said her dad. "Want another carrot?"

Grace, back up in her bedroom, curled up with Idol on the bed. Thinking she'd better test the water, she called Lindsey on her cell phone.

"Hi," Lindsey said. "Where you been?"

"Oh, just hanging around. Got an A-plus on my essay."

"You're getting to be a serious nerd. Don't know about you, Gracie."

"Got some news. You know those two girls I told you about at the Dome?"

"Yeah, with the weird names—like wine?"

"Essence and Chardonnai," Grace filled in. "Well, they're going to be staying with us for a while."

"Us? Who's *us*?"

"Us. The Woodson family."

"You've got to be kidding. Sister Joan called my parents to ask if we could take some kids in, but my stepmom said no. She says she sees nothing but trouble coming. First time I've heard her make sense."

"Trouble?"

"They're not like us."

"But..."

"They're black refugees."

"They need help."

"Who are you? Atticus? That's a book. He isn't real. My dad says let well enough alone."

Then Lindsey cut her off, something about homework. Had to go. Grace stared at the cell phone. Lindsey's dad was a lawyer. How could he think like that? What had she gotten herself into? She reached across the bed to the small table and grabbed her journal. Idol looked up at her, and then settled back against her stomach, purring. "Idol," Grace said, petting her softly, "stay close. I'm going to need you."

ESSENCE Journal
September 5, 2005

Mimmi's dead. Dr. Woodson told me today. And I don't even know if she was buried anywhere. She always said folks needed a proper burial with a jazz parade or they would never rest in peace. You out there somewhere, Mimmi?

I guess George was a hero trying to save her, but it didn't work, and now George is still lost. I am very sad and haven't told Chardonnai yet. I just keep crying and when she asks why I am crying, Mrs. Beaudrie tries to get her little mind on other things. She bought her a new doll. Chardonnai calls her Mama and rocks her

NOLA Gals/Barbara J. Rebbeck

in her arms. Maybe I should ask the trumpet man if he is my dad now as me and Chardonnai have no more grandmama and could sure use a daddy.

So here's what Dr. Woodson tells me George did. Yes sir that skinny French mutt was a real hero. Mimmi would have laughed till she shook all over. She had this tremendous laugh that rocked up from her belly and her eyes would just get all sparkly when she was happy. She said me and Char brought her a bird of happiness that just sat itself on her shoulder. Cept when we were ornery and got on Mimmi's last nerve. Anyways we left Mimmi up in Mama's bedroom and we still don't know what happened to Mama either. Well, we went in the boat with the two men. We didn't want to leave her but she tricked us. Told us white lies. They took us to a big bridge with so many people there that Char was so scared she bawled her eyes out. Later men went back and painted on the wall of the house with special numbers that meant Mimmi still was up there with George. Well, I guess George got bored, and out the window he jumped his skinny butt. He was swimming around in that nasty water quite a ways from the old white house when up came another boat and tried to fetch him in. But oh no, stubborn old George just kept swimming the other way and barking his head off loud enough to wake the dead Mimmi would say. George got on her last nerve sometimes too. So the boat just took off following him. George led them back to our house. They saw the marks on the wall and tried to rescue Mimmi, but she was already dead. Must have been the diabetes that took her. So they left her there and changed the mark on the wall to say she was dead and they could wait a while to get her. They tried to get George into the boat but he insisted still to stay guarding Mimmi. And that's how Mimmi died. And I don't know if she's still in that old white house or not. I hope not. And who knows where old George ended up. He was a hero.

Dr. Woodson says me and Chardonnai can come live with him and his wife and Grace for a while. I want to stay with Mrs. Beaudrie and Harold but I guess there's not enough room in the apartment they are going to. Dr. Woodson says his wife is real nice. I guess she's a vet and takes care of animals. Maybe she can find George or get me another dog. Grace has a cat named Idol. Maybe she will love me. I will go to school with Grace. Chardonnai too. It all seems so strange. I feel lost. Old Harold is playing that song again about missing New Orleans. I sure do. Goodbye Mimmi. Where are you Mama? I'll take care of me and Chardonnai. I hope someone is watching over you. I can't write any more. The tears are coming fast and dropping onto these pages. And they're all wet. I'm so upset. I need Mimmi to tell me a truth. Tell me it's gonna be okay.

GRACE

"You've got to be kidding," Lindsey said. She was sitting out in the school courtyard, a small group of loyal friends surrounding her. They were a little wave of blue plaid, cascading down in the shade of the large Chinaberry planted years ago in the honor of some major cash donor. Careful to avoid the poisonous yellow fruit fallen from the tree, they sat around in bunches, chatting and gossiping.

"Why not invite them over?" Grace asked, her eyes on the two lone girls across the pathway, near the statue of Saint Catherine.

"Oh, do what you want," replied Lindsey," but I'm outa here, now." Jumping up, she motioned for her little clique to follow, and they made their way to the side door, like ducklings following their mom.

Now alone herself, Grace headed over to the two girls. As she approached, Essence looked up at her from her bench near the statue. She was sitting with another "Katrina refugee" as the media called them. Frozen, they appeared to be new statues added to the little shrine.

"You don't have to hang with us," said Essence. "Me and Sofia are fine."

"Don't be silly," said Grace. "And don't let those girls bother you."

"They sure don't seem to be very friendly to us. The teachers keep saying what fine girls they all are, but I don't know," said Sofia, standing up and brushing her skirt off. Both girls were dressed in hand-me-down uniforms, picked from the re-sale rack in the basement store. The skirts showed wear and tear; Sofia's had a very uneven hem. She was living with another family not far from where Grace lived. "And I had better clothes than this raggedy skirt back home. NOLA gals dress fine."

As the girls moved toward the door to the stairwell, they heard someone rapping on a classroom window in the primary school. Looking over, they saw little Chardonnai, her nose pressed up against the window, her fingers tapping out a beat. She was screwing her face all up and crossing her eyes in what she called her "ugly face," hoping to get a laugh out of her sister. Essence shook her head, smiled, and perked up, trying to appear happy for her sister. She gave a big wave and Char smiled back.

"It's easier for her," Essence said. "She don't know what's going on. Too little to take it all in. But I wish she wouldn't cry so much."

"Has she made any friends?" Grace asked. Mostly Chardonnai stayed in her room with Essence when they were home with the Woodson family. Her parents had intended that each of the girls would have their own bedroom; but the first night after lights were out, Chardonnai had crept into Essence's room, and they had found her asleep the next morning curled up on the floor in her new soft pink nightgown and fuzzy bunny slippers, clutching the wedding quilt. "The sleep of angels," her mom had called it. So now the two girls shared a room, saying there was plenty room for the two of them in the single bed. The single bed was just fine. Just cozy.

"She's made a few friends, mostly New Orleans gals. I think

the younger girls accept us better," said Essence, her head down, almost as if she were counting the steps to the doorway.

"I sure wish we could go home," Sofia said, "I miss everyone so much. NOLA. NOLA. NOLA. You're the finest city in the world."

"Yes, ma'am, even if you are underwater," Essence sighed.

The two girls had not known each other before the hurricane as they had lived in different wards in the city and gone to different schools. Sofia's mom was with her, making it easier for her to adjust in some ways. She had a temporary job in the school cafeteria which did not help though. Sofia knew the girls talked behind her back, and when she had to go through the cafeteria line, she was well aware of the exaggerated comments and rolled eyes as her mom handed the girls their choices for lunch. "Lettuce lady," they called her.

Essence dreaded going back into the building from the calm courtyard. It was the not knowing that was the worse to accept. Why were these girls so mean? Could she do anything to make them like her? Didn't they care she'd lost Mimmi, George, and a big old white house?

"Grace, what about those goals and values you girls are always reading out loud?" asked Essence. "They're posted on every wall in every classroom. They say you love each other and look out for each other. Sister Joan gave me a little book with the values all listed in it. She said you live by these values, but I don't see it. If you did believe, I thought you would be kind at this school. Where's your faith? Where's good will towards men and little girls?"

"Yes," said Grace, "this situation is a real test of us all."

"Well, if you ask me, most of the girls are failing that test," said Essence, her voice breaking.

Embarrassed for her friends, Grace pulled open the door, only to find herself face to face with Sister Joan.

"Ladies," Sister Joan said, with her usual vigor, "how goes it?"

"Oh, we're just fine," Sofia said, hoping to dissolve into the tile.

"Grace, you're living the goals. Good for you," Sister added, her hand moving to the large cross she always wore around her neck. She bustled on as she always did, in a hurry and a flurry of activity. She had to be the busiest, most committed nun in the world.

Walking up the stairs to French class, Essence sighed and said, "I just read the part in *Mockingbird* where the neighbor lady tells Scout and Jem that some people are just born to do our unpleasant jobs. To be Christian for us all like Atticus. I reckon that's you, Grace, and your parents. Even fuzzy old Idol. You're Christians for us all. Funny that folks think that's unpleasant."

"But being your friend is not unpleasant at all," said Grace, trying to look straight ahead to avoid seeing Essence's slumped baby steps towards Sister Grenier's classroom.

As Sofia walked into the room of girls, their chatter fell silent, all faces just staring at her. "Nothing unpleasant about this silence. No, ma'am, nothing at all," she said, turning back to Grace and Essence who followed behind.

They took their seats and faced forward as Sister began today's lesson. "*Conjugez, mes filles,*" she insisted.

"*J'aime, tu aimes, elle aime.*

Nous aimons, vous aimez, elles aiment."

"Ah, yes. *Mais oui,*" Grace muttered. "We do love each other."

Sofia rolled her eyes and recited, whispering "We do know our French in NOLA, Grace. Why, yes, we do indeed. *Bien sûr* I can just smell the *beignets* in the bakeries."

"*Encore, mes filles,*" intoned Sister Grenier. And so it went on and on.

ESSENCE Journal
September 7, 2005

I miss Mama and Mimmi so much. I am trying to be brave and do my best at school but it is so hard. I have to set an example for Chardonnai. I have even taken to giving her truths just like Mimmi. We got to be strong I keep telling her. No one can really help us but us. We got to be happy as a NOLA Mardi Gras parade. We got to be sweet as NOLA beignets. (That's a donut for you in Houston but a very special yummy one!) We got to be cool as NOLA jazz. Yes ma'am, little Char. We got to survive. I'm almost done reading Mockingbird. That writer Harper Lee is so good. I feel like she sees right inside me. I wish I could meet her or talk to her. Maybe by writing this book she was doing more unpleasant jobs for us. Sometimes, I cry when I think that the girls and their parents—well, some of them think of little Char as unpleasant. I can cope for me but looking at that child, my sister as "ugly" or a "job" upsets me a lot.

Here's a strange happening. I have to share a locker with Grace. So after lunch I went to get my copy of Mockingbird to read outside by the shrine. I like reading there by myself. I feel safe there and you'd laugh, but I talk real quiet to St. Cat. About being a ghost, about Chardonnai, about feeling unpleasant and being a black girl. I know St. Cat is a stone statue but maybe she can hear.

So I opened my locker and was feeling around for my French book, when I noticed a tiny little package. I backed off and looked around me but there was no one in the hallway. I must say I was afraid of what might be in that tiny package as I knew there were plenty of girls who would have put a voodoo spell on me as fast as they could. Almost as if they had a new school goal now to hate me. But Mimmi always said that curiosity killed the cat until satisfaction brought him back, so closing my eyes and thinking about friendly Idol I reached for the package. Opening my eyes I turned it over and over. Afraid yet wanting to know. Just

NOLA Gals/Barbara J. Rebbeck

then that bratty girl Madison pushed past me, knocking me into the locker on purpose. She thinks she's so cool and popular. All the cool girls roll up their plaid skirts when Sister Joan isn't around so's you can almost see their behinds. They wear a lot of make-up too. Sometimes the nuns make them go scrub their faces clean, but they just put the goop back on. Mimmi always told me I was pretty enough without painting up my face. But these rich girls like all that. They even have painted up hair. Eyes lined in black like big holes. Brushed cheeks and red lips. I looked up at Madison, just sure what Mimmi would say if she had to meet this painted up girl.

"Oh sorry," she said, "I didn't see you there."

A ghost I thought. She's making me invisible. She hurried on before I could try to say anything to her, her behind waving back at me. I pulled my attention back to the package in my hand. Got to be strong. I unwrapped the silver paper real careful so's not to rip it. I started bawling when I looked down at two sticks of gum inside the wrapper. Just like in the book when Jem had found stuff in that old tree knothole. Secret presents from a secret sender. It must be a kind gift. I let go my breath I'd been holding in. I understood it wasn't just gum, it was love. Vous aimez.

GRACE

"Adults have a way of telling themselves everything is just fine when it comes to kids," said Grace. She was in her Advisee Group which met for twenty minutes each morning to discuss issues and problems. She looked around her at the nine other girls, hoping for some support. Silence and stony stares were all that came back at her. Two of the girls even had their music streaming into their ears. She tried again. "I try to imagine teachers at meetings, never really cutting deep enough to even scrape the truth; or, you know, parents sitting on patios, tired after a day's work, sipping on their cocktails, smug about us, their perfect daughters."

"So you think this is all a sham?" asked her favorite teacher, Ms. Rodgers. She was a bit of a rebel. Not a nun, not even Catholic. She was a rule breaker and a great teacher.

"Sometimes, yes," Grace hesitated again, looking around the group for help."Any other opinions?" urged Ms. Rodgers

The girls stared back at her, not wanting to involve

NOLA Gals/Barbara J. Rebbeck

themselves in a conversation that didn't compare the latest designer bag or someone's new shoes or Friday's dance. "Well then, it's time to write. We have a few minutes for you to put down your thoughts on paper for me," said Ms. Rodgers.

"About what?" Lindsey asked, "I guess I wasn't listening." She'd had her back turned while Grace spoke, whispering to Madison. Things had certainly changed with Grace and Lindsey since the arrival of the New Orleans gals. They seldom spoke, and this admission on Lindsey's part really stung Grace.

"Grace was saying that things are happening here with our New Orleans guests that the adults in this school are not aware of. Let me hear what you think," Ms. Rodgers repeated. Sitting down at her desk, she began to write, cueing the girls to begin.

GRACE WOODSON
Journal

I believe that the girls from New Orleans are having a rough time adjusting. It's been hard enough for them to be plopped here in Houston after all they endured in New Orleans. The two girls staying with me have lost their grandmother and are still searching for their mom. They have been uprooted from everything they know and love, dressed in hand-me-down uniforms and marched off to school. They are not even Catholic. While the adults are patting themselves on the back for being so charitable, (I can't help but think of the deadly old ladies of To Kill a Mockingbird) the students here at St. Catherine's are burying every goal we recite as they casually kick or shove these girls, utter smears under their breaths, or in their hearts, just want them out. "They are not our kind," they say. Adults need to listen. Please listen.

LINDSEY TOWNSEND
Journal

I really don't know what Grace is talking about. I think we have done our best to welcome those people. Why should we all disrupt our lives to make theirs better? It was okay at first, but now it's time for them to go back home. They don't have any money anyway so what difference does it make where they live? A trailer will do fine. And please, don't let them come to the dance. That will ruin everything. Can you imagine what they'll wear? Grace has become some kind of crusader. She doesn't care about her real friends anymore. Can we talk about something else now? This is getting old. And another thing, in Grace's new bible, *Mockingbird*, most white people are lousy and cruel while all the blacks are angels. Give me a break.

SISTER JOAN

She looked up from her cluttered desk and the report she was preparing for the Board of Directors on the NOLA guests. She had the feeling someone was watching her. She was right. Chardonnai stood in the doorway, clutching a little plastic bag. She was clearly uncomfortable, twisting one little leg around the other like a pelican about to lose her balance.

"Come in. Come in," Sister Joan said. "What can I do for you?"

Chardonnai hesitated, but moved a few steps into the room, looking all around her at all the books. "I never seen so many books. You must be a smart and important person, Sister Joan."

Chardonnai edged closer to Sister Joan, not sure she belonged near such an important white lady. She stood nearer, her head bowed trying to be as polite as she could be: "As sweet as a beignet," Essence would say.

"What have you got there, Char?"

"This here bag?"

"Yes, that bag, Char. What's in it? Looks like some dirt."

"Oh, no, Sister. What's in this bag is what's left... I mean Essence says the remains of Mimmi."

Sister Joan jumped up in spite of herself, wondering if this small child was telling her the truth. She knew her grandmother had died in the hurricane. Maybe Char was playing a game.

"Where did you find the...remains?" she asked.

"When we got home from school, there was a package sitting on the counter in the kitchen. Linda, the cook—she is soooo nice—told me to wait till Mrs. Woodson came home from work to open it. She said the package had two names on it. Me and Essence."

"And then what?"

"Well, Mrs. Woodson came home. She picked me up and sat me on her lap. I was polite as could be cuz I never sat on no white woman before. She said we would wait for Essence and drink lemonade first. Sure was tasty and so cool."

"And when Essence came home?"

"She knew something was up for me to be sitting with a white lady so she got some cool lemonade and sat her butt down beside us. She asked what could be in that package."

"And did Mrs. Woodson let you open it?"

"She reached right over me and started to cut the package open where there was tape. Then she opened the box and inside was a plain cardboard box. Nothing special to me. I had to slide my glass over to the side before I spilled the lemonade all over the box."

"And what did Essence do?"

"She leaned over and looked at the box, then picked up a card that was attached to the box. 'Lord a mercy,' she said. 'This says it's Mimmi.'"

"'Yes,' Mrs. Woodson said, 'these are the remains of Mimmi.'

"'Uh, huh,' I said. 'Her big butt would not fit in that itty-bitty box. She would say anyone tried to stuff her in that box would surely be on her last nerve.'"

"But these are just tiny parts of her," Sister Joan told her.

"We have to put her some place holy so she can rest in peace. The only place I know is here where the statue of beautiful Saint Cat is. Can I, Sister? Can we let her rest in the court?"

"Don't you want to take her home to NOLA?" Sister asked, holding back tears, moved by the love this tiny girl had for Mimmi.

"Essence put some ashes away to take back home when we go and we will go, right?"

"Of course you will."

Just then old Harold stuck his head in the doorway. He carried his trumpet. A beam of sunshine caught its light from the window.

"Can Harold play Mimmi's song when we put her in the court?"

"Of course. But what about Essence?"

"Essence said she would wait for New Orleans. Char just couldn't wait," Harold said.

"Essence say she don't want Mimmi here at all where the girls are so mean to her," Char said, half afraid to tell Sister this big truth.

"But we love you girls," Sister Joan replied. "It'll get better. You'll see."

"Ma'am, we need to put Mimmi at peace right now. Right here. Come on, Sister," she said as she grabbed Sister Joan's hand, still clutching the bag in her other hand close to her heart. "Mimmi say no voodoo doodads, just Christian love."

The trio of mourners headed out the door and down the hall into the quiet courtyard. St. Cat as usual held out her arms to them.

"Does it matter that Mimmi wasn't Catholic?" Char asked.

"No, dear, not at all," said Sister Joan as she watched Char kneel down before the statue and open the little bag.

"I know Mimmi is with Jesus," Char said, filling her little hand with the ashes of her grandmother. Now, Harold," she said, "play that tune as sweet as molasses."

Harold filled the air with Mimmi's favorite tune and as Char sprinkled the ashes on the ground before St. Cat, she could see Mimmi rise and float up her lazy, lazy river.

ESSENCE Journal
September 10, 2005

So little Chardonnai scattered Mimmi's ashes in the courtyard in front of the statue of St. Cat. Not all of them. I promise, Mimmi we will get some of you back to New Orleans. Harold played his trumpet. I didn't want to see it. I would have cried and just upset Char. Sister Joan was nice to let her do it. She's a good lady. Can you call a nun a lady?

So things are going okay I guess. Some of the girls at school hate me, but I can be strong for Mimmi. I got to remember her truths. I got to look after Chardonnai. The Woodsons are

Barbara J. Rebbeck/NOLA Gals

good people. Just today Dr. Woodson asked me if I wanted to go to a baseball game. It seems Grace and him love the Astros and they are really doing good this year. He says they may even make it to the World Series. But I couldn't stop thinking about how it would feel to go into another dome. I think I've been in enough of those for the rest of my life. Makes me shake all over just to even think of myself there. That's why I didn't want to go.

I've been thinking more and more about Mrs. Beaudrie and the trumpet man. I haven't seen them since we've been here. She called me once and said they were fine in their new apartment. Trouble is they got no car or way to get here to see us. Maybe if I ask Dr. Woodson they could go get them and bring them over. Maybe it's time to get it straight about Harold. If he is my daddy. Char got him to come play the trumpet for Mimmi.

Funny thing. I always hated writing at school. It was so boring. The teachers gave us dumb topics like what we did all summer. Alls I ever did was sit on the porch or take George for a walk or mind Char. But since I read Miss Harper Lee's story about Scout and her troubles I try to write better myself. Sometimes I read parts of her book again just watching how she put the words on the page. She is a teacher to me. Then I try to write like her with better words and about deep thoughts.

NOLA Gals/Barbara J. Rebbeck

Anyway Grace says there's a big dance this Friday after school. And you don't have to wear a uniform. She said her mama would surely buy me a new outfit for the dance if I want. I heard Madison and Lindsey saying that no New Orleans girls should go to the dance. That we weren't wanted. Sometimes it's scary being at school. Other times it's fine. Like when I found another gift in my locker today. It was a CD of Louis Armstrong songs. I hurried home and Grace let me play it on the old boom box in the basement. I played it once—then again, closing my eyes and flying right back to Bourbon Street. There we all were, Mimmi, Mama, Char, even old George just strutting along in a Second Line parade. Floats were coming on down the street with Zulu members tossing out throws to the crowds, lots of purple and green beads flying through the air being caught and tossed around people's arms and necks. And at the head of the parade marched my daddy, Harold, the sun shining off his trumpet, his feet stepping to that New Orleans beat as he moved his way right through the city.

See, I'm trying hard to write like a grownup lady. I wrote that last part over and over with lots of cross-outs till I really liked it. Then I copied it all over again so neat I surprised myself. Ms., Rodgers is showing me where the commas go. Mimmi would be proud. That's a truth.

GRACE

Grace was upset, probably as angry as she'd ever been. She'd been trying to make Essence feel wanted at school by leaving secret gifts for her like the ones for Scout and Jem. She knew that Essence had loved the Satchmo CD, and she must have had a light heart when she opened their locker today only to jump back, screaming. Everyone had come running, seeing Essence bent over double, her head down, her knees sagging.

"Essence," Sister Joan had asked as she stopped, headed down the hall to her office, "are you hurt? What's wrong?"

Pointing her hand up towards the locker, still averting her eyes, she cried out, "Look. They hate me."

The ladies of St. Cat's, gathered together, stared into the locker to see a small poster with the bold letters *White Power* scrawled across it. A knife pierced the heart which encircled the letters. Sister Joan ripped the poster from the locker and put it under her arm.

NOLA Gals/Barbara J. Rebbeck

"Girls," Sister said urgently, "go to the chapel now. I cannot believe this has happened in our school."

Grace knew this was very serious. Finally the adults would listen. The only times they were ever summoned to the chapel were in times of great crisis.

The girls hurried along, news of the poster spreading through the hallway. Hushed by teachers standing at the chapel doors, they waited outside. Sister Joan appeared in the doorway and walked into the center aisle and laid the poster on the floor. Turning, she beckoned for the girls to come into the chapel. One by one they walked over the poster, taking seats in the pews. Bowing their heads in prayer, they waited for Sister Joan to appear at the altar. She came alone, waiting for their teachers to be seated. The poster, now scuffed and torn, still lay on the floor in the aisle. At the altar she stood in silence, her head bowed for a few seconds. She did not want the girls to see she was fighting back tears. Raising her head, she began to pace slowly, stopping and staring into the eyes of each girl in the front row. Finding her calm voice, she asked, "Essence and Grace, will you bring the poster up to the altar?"

Normally, the girls would be asked to bring the gifts of bread and wine forward to the waiting priest, so the two stepped from the back of the chapel and began the familiar journey to Sister Joan. As they moved, Grace was aware of all the pews of girls and teachers looking up from prayer and staring at the evil poster Grace held above her head. Essence followed behind her, tears soaking her cheeks and dripping to the collar of her uniform blouse. Sister Joan began to sing in a low steady voice the hymn *Amazing Grace*. A gasp went up from the older girls who had studied the Civil War and knew the story behind the hymn written by a reformed slave trader. One by one the girls joined the singing and their voices rose as one to the very top of the chapel echoing down to the stained glass windows. When the hymn ended, they all knelt as Grace handed the poster to Sister Joan. Gesturing to Essence, Sister pointed to a large silver bowl she had placed on a small wooden table behind the altar. Essence wadded up the poster and placed it in the bowl as Grace lit a match from an altar candle. Then Sister Joan lit the poster and all three stood back to watch it burn. A ripple of applause began from the back of the chapel, spreading like the fire from pew to pew. In silence everyone watched the flames devour the poster, reducing it to red embers.

"Go back to class, girls." Sister said. "Let this dying fire give birth in its embers to new tolerance and love for those here and in New Orleans."

Throughout the chapel, soft sobs could be heard from many girls as they filed out, returning to class.

School was dismissed early. An emergency e-mail went out to all parents. And the dance was canceled. The adults were indeed listening. But in their efforts to counteract the poster had they just made it worse for the New Orleans guests? Grace wondered.

Since Grace's mom and dad were not available to pick them up, Grace, Essence, and Chardonnai shared a ride home with Lindsey's stepmom. It was a silent ride. No one spoke. As Mrs. Townsend drove up the drive to Grace's house, Chardonnai began to squiggle around in her seatbelt, her nose pressed against the window. "Look," she cried out, "It's Mrs. Beaudrie."

"Oh," said Mrs. Townsend. "Another one of those people."

Grace shot her a half-wondering look, one of those I'm-keeping-my-mouth-shut-because-you're-an-adult glares and reached for the door handle. They jumped out of the car, Chardonnai leaping up the path, Essence not far behind.

Grace closed the car door and leaned into the open window to thank Mrs. Townsend for the ride.

Mrs. Townsend leaned towards Grace, pulling her sunglasses off and staring her right in the eyes across the front seat. She gestured to Lindsey, sitting next to her and said, "Grace, Lindsey tells me you're becoming quite the little activist. Be careful, my dear. The adults in this suburb have built a community we are very proud of. We shall preserve it. Say hello to your mom and dad." Lindsey stared straight ahead, burning a hole through the windshield, determined to ignore her former

BFF. Grace shrugged her shoulders and took a few steps away from the car.

The Cadillac dissolved into a cloud of dust as it sped down the drive, leaving a stunned Grace looking after it. She turned to see a joyous reunion on the porch as the two girls and Mrs. Beaudrie danced some crazy jig together, laughing and holding hands. "I'd rather be with 'those people,'" Grace said under her breath.

THOSE PEOPLE

"Mrs. Beaudrie," she cried as she walked up the drive. "How'd you get here?"

"Child, I found me the right bus that got me almost here, and then I walked these old bones the rest of the weary way. Just had to see my two gals. But I sure could use a drink of water about now, Gracie."

"Of course," Grace said, fumbling for her keys in her book bag. "Come on in."

The little group hurried into the hallway and then on to the kitchen. Linda had left the mail on the counter, and Grace picked up the pile of envelopes to leaf through them. She was hoping to see a response to the letter she'd written to Carrie Underwood what seemed ages ago now. She felt like she was living a totally different life from that carefree girl who had so recently giggled with Lindsey on the patio about the latest gossip.

"So what you girls been up to? I hope you're not giving the Woodsons any trouble. They're such nice folk." Mrs. Beaudrie had found a comfy spot and now was perched on a kitchen stool, the two girls on either side of her, arms locked around each other. Grace thought they looked like one of their magnolia trees; Mrs. Beaudrie in a bright flowered dress, the girls like a plaid blanket spread beneath.

"Things aren't so good at school," Essence began, her voice soft.

"You mean those rich girls know more about reading and writing than you. You can catch up if you work real hard. Look how fast you read that mockingbird book. I liked that story so much. I miss hearing Gracie read to us all. That was about the only good thing that came out of being in that dome," Mrs. Beaudrie said, leaning over closer to Essence and giving her a hug.

"The girls just don't want us there," shouted out Chardonnai, fighting tears. "They say bad things to us, and they left an awful sign in Grace's locker."

"Why, Gracie, what is this poor child going on about? This can't be true."

"Not everyone feels that way. But there are a few girls and their parents who think you all have stayed long enough and need to go home now," Grace said, hoping to play down the seriousness of the problem.

"Home to what? They must have TVs in their fancy houses. They must have seen the flooding, the floating bodies, the rotten water," replied Mrs. Beaudrie. She pulled Chardonnai onto her lap, hugging her even closer.

Grace looked back at the mail in her hand and flipped an envelope to the back of the pile to reveal a legal-sized envelope addressed to her. Putting the rest of the pile down on the counter, she turned it and ripped it open. She pulled out a single sheet of paper, unfolded it and gasped as she read "*Get rid of them.*" The words bled across the page in red ink. Shocked, Grace dropped the paper on the counter and jumped back, recoiling as if someone had spit in her face.

Mrs. Beaudrie said, "What's wrong, child? You look like you've seen a ghost."

"Yes, a mockingbird ghost," Grace said, holding up the paper.

"See," said Essence, crying again. "They don't want us here at all."

Chardonnai began her wail again, too, looking to the ceiling, asking for her mama and her Mimmi.

Essence calmed herself and said softly, "Is that trumpet man still with you? He hasn't run out on you?"

Mrs. Beaudrie looked puzzled and said, "Of course not. Harold is a good man. Why, he goes every night to play in the jazz clubs downtown. He don't get paid no money, but he says it's just a matter of time before the right man hears him play his magic and offers him a job on the spot. And look how he played for Mimmi's ashes at Saint Cat's. Why you asking?"

"Harold? You say?" Essence asked, making sure of his name before she said what she had guessed. She would do this for Chardonnai, she thought. For peace of mind and for her future.

"Course he's Harold," said Mrs. Beaudrie, pushing the girls away and standing up. "Where's that water you promised, Gracie?"

Grace moved across to the large refrigerator, opened it, and gestured for Mrs. Beaudrie to make a choice from the pop, lemonade, sweet ice tea, bottled water, or beer.

"Lordy, you girls have got it made here, judging from the likes of this huge refrigerator," she laughed, lightening the mood. Grabbing the pitcher of sweet tea, she asked Grace for glasses for everybody.

Grace got the glasses from the cupboard and found chips to snack on, too. As she poured them into a bowl, she said, "Let's go into the living room." Rummaging in the refrigerator, she came up with a jar of salsa and some ranch dip. Curious where Essence was going with her questions about Harold, she led them into the next room. Mrs. Beaudrie stopped them all, insisting they first remove their shoes. Then she claimed the couch, the girls again on either side of her. Grace put the snacks down on the table, offering a coaster to everyone and sat on a leather tuft facing the three.

"So what's this curiosity about Harold, Essence?" Mrs. Beaudrie asked, wriggling her toes in the soft beige carpet.

"Well," Essence hesitated.

"Lord, girl, just spit it out," Mrs. Beaudrie urged, her eyes locked on Essence as if to prevent her from running.

"I think Harold is my daddy," Essence almost shouted, her eyes closed tight.

"Mine, too?" Chardonnai asked, reaching over and poking Essence hard in the stomach.

"Ouch," she yelled, hitting back at Chardonnai with a softened punch.

"*Mon Dieu*! Stop it, you two," laughed Mrs. Beaudrie, separating them and pushing them back into the soft couch.

"Explain," Grace commanded, with a severe tone that gave Essence no choice.

Reaching into her blouse pocket, Essence pulled out a crumpled photo. Smoothing it with her hand, she showed it to Mrs. Beaudrie and said, "Isn't this Harold?"

Mrs. Beaudrie took it and held it out a distance from her face, and said, "My eyes ain't what they used to be, but I do declare there is a definite resemblance of Harold to this young man with his horn."

Grace, from her viewpoint, could see the back of the photo and said, "There's something written on the back."

Flipping it over, Mrs. Beaudrie said, "Bless me, it does say one word: *Harold*. Where'd you get this, child?" she asked turning to Essence.

"I found it in our shed, in a big box of stuff. I knew that must be the daddy my mama always talked about who could melt you with music sticky as molasses. I hid it in my room under my mattress. It was the only thing I rescued before Katrina took everything else, even Mimmi. Maybe George. Maybe even Mama."

RITA

1 n a depression, she rises east of the Bahamas on the trail of her sister, heading for the Florida Keys. Below her, tiny cars clog the freeways, fleeing. Not again, they think. On a whim, she bypasses the Keys, her anger churning as she rises over the Gulf of Mexico, her fury at new heights, venting record winds at her recalcitrant sibling. Not again. New Orleans and Texas lay ahead. Her chance to best her sister at last.

As the hours pass, she continues her vendetta in the guise of finding her sister. She knows in her heart that she cannot do that, for Katrina is long gone, leaving others to clean up her mess as usual. Her hatred of her sister weakens her as she barrels towards shore, veering left then right, lost in her own drenched clouds. Her white gown is soaked through and through, twisted around her in a hopeless twirl. Again, beneath her, she sees the tiny trucks, buses, and cars in a long slow parade to anywhere out of her rage. Not again, they say.

Early morning and she comes ashore, lost, making landfall somewhere near the Texas-Louisiana border. Huge with her pain, she pulls trees up, tears roofs off, and floods buildings with her tears. Sobbing,

NOLA Gals/Barbara J. Rebbeck

surging, she re-breaks levees only just partially sandbagged after her sister's fit in New Orleans. Through her swollen eyes, she watches as the wards flood again. Slowing, energy drained, she passes by, sparing Houston. Whimpering, confused, she begins to fade.

"Yes, again. Oh, yes again. I am Rita," *she calls out with her last breath.*

ESSENCE Journal
September 27, 2005

Not again they all thought. But they were wrong. Hurricane Rita hit hard again. And I bet our old shotgun house is probably underwater again. The water gurgling up against the guillotine window, and the old iron gates all rusted and bent. We still have no word from Mama or even George again. Too many agains for me. Pitiful goings on. When Rita was smashing her way to Houston, the Woodsons decided to stay and wait her out. Both of them worried about their patients, especially all the animals at the shelter. They helped get others out of nursing homes and hospitals, but said

NOLA Gals/Barbara J. Rebbeck

we'd probably be okay since we weren't in the real lowland area. Turns out they were right. But it was scary waiting. I prayed a lot even if I'm not Catholic. Folks who tried to go were all jammed up on the roads, running out of gas, not even knowing where they were headed for sure. It was a real mess on TV. Wolf Blitzer and me are friends by now cuz I watch him so often for any news from New Orleans. It's like he's my grandpa, giving me bad news.

So we have time off school for a few days. This is good because kids there still don't like us. When Rita was on her way, they were all saying probably more of us would come now, and they'd never have a dance again. They still don't know who's leaving the mean notes for us.

Turns out Harold *is* my daddy. After I told Mrs. Beaudrie what I guessed about him, she told Grace's parents and we all got together for a little reunion. I felt sorry for Char because now I have a daddy and she don't. Harold says he ain't her daddy and she needs to ask Mama about all that. He says he's sure that ol gal will show up sometime. He says no hurricane will beat her. I'm still living here until Harold can get a job. He's still playing his trumpet in town bars for free, hoping for a job offer. Then I will go live with him. I guess Char will come, too. At least that's what the adults tell me. Who knows the truth? Katrina and Rita have drowned most all of Mimmi's truths and even Mimmi.

GRACE

Much to everyone's relief, especially the girls from New Orleans, Sister had at last relented and announced they might try a dance after a two-week probation. Grace thought Sister Joan had felt doubly sorry for the girls after Hurricane Rita had hit, plunging them back into the waves of worry and grief they had tried to survive just a month ago. Grace had mixed feelings about the event. She was happy that the Katrina girls were off the hook as parents and students had made them the scapegoats for the dance cancellation. But she was also nervous because she was not exactly a favorite among her friends at the moment. Her support for Essence and her friends had distanced her from her own circle. Curled up on her bed, Idol purring beside her, she was in a struggle with her French verbs again. Getting nowhere, she slammed the text shut and reached for her iPod. A little Carrie music was just the thing to soothe her worries now. Idol rose up, licking Grace's face playfully. She pulled her down next to her, hoping she'd stretch out beside her for a short nap. Later she was going to the mall with her mom and Essence to pick out new outfits for the dance. Maybe they'd have a little peace for a few days.

From next door in Essence's room, notes of a trumpet solo drifted through the wall. Missing New Orleans again. The CD Grace had hidden in their locker was playing, soothing Essence she thought. It had been only a few days ago that Grace's mom and dad had arranged a meeting with Essence and Harold—a reunion of sorts. It turned out that old Harold had been clueless to the fact that his daughter had been right in front of him for weeks now. Or at least that's what he claimed. He had cried. Essence had cried. Char had cried. And finally, they'd all just had a good cry. Char's parentage was still doubtful, but that would be another story. Grace's dad had been trying unsuccessfully to find the girls' mama. Essence had given up on her, too, and now was very concerned over Char's future.

"She's got to stay with us," she insisted to Grace's parents. "You've got to tell Harold that. He'll listen to you."

"Don't panic," Dr. Woodson had told her. "We're looking for your mother. Until we know more, both of you will stay right here."

Harold had agreed to this arrangement as he was still waiting for that first paying gig to appear. "I appreciate your kindness, sir," he'd said, hugging both the girls as they sat on either side of him on the couch. "It's time I take responsibility. I just need a little more time. I'm in touch with a friend of mine still living in the French Quarter who says the bars will be opening back up soon's you know it. There will be jobs then. Folks who work there will be put up at the city hotels for awhile. I bet you girls would love to go back home, right?"

Essence broke free from her hug and looked Harold in the eye and said, "I'd love to see the back of that school, but could you be a good daddy and not run off again?"

Harold laughed, "Essence, honey, don't you sound like your mama and Mimmi!"

***

The Carrie ringtone woke her from her dream. In her dream, she'd been lounging on the patio with Lindsey, a bit tipsy from the liquor they'd stolen from the Tiki bar. Talking, dissing, and laughing. Things had been easy in her dream. She reached for her phone, dumping Idol on the floor. Dazed, she read the caller ID, and sat up straight, surprised at the name.

"Hi, Grace. What's up?"

"Jack?" Grace asked.

"So I guess things have been a little rough lately?"

"Not too bad. I'm learning a lot."

"So I thought you might want to go to the dance with me tomorrow," Jack asked with his usual confidence.

All Grace could see was Lindsey killing her. She imagined Lindsey pulling her under in her own pool, drowning her. "What about Lindsey?" she asked, hesitating.

"You know, all this stuff about the New Orleans students has made me think again about everyone. Lindsay has acted like an ass too many times."

"Well, she's not even talking to me now," Grace continued.

"And if you go with me, us walking in together won't help any," Jack warned.

"Maybe she won't show," Grace said.

"Well, what do you think?"

"I think I'm in deep enough. But why not?" Grace giggled, poking her toe into Idol's soft belly. Her laugh dissolved into guilt though as she thought about what she was doing to her best friend. Was she being a silly teen betraying her friend for a guy?

"I'll talk to you later about how we'll get there," Jack said. There was a long pause, and Grace thought he was gone. But his voice came back. "Grace?"

"Yes?"

"You must...I mean you probably know that Lindsey was behind the White Power poster and the note to you in the mail," Jack said.

Grace said nothing at first. She knew how Sister had tried hard to get someone to admit to the racist incidents, but the clique of ladies had stood firm, protecting each other, mouths closed. Even the parents had rallied together, determined their children not suffer because of the New Orleans refugees.

"Are you sure?" Grace said, her heart racing fast.

"She told me. Madison helped her."

"Would you tell Sister?"

"I'd have to think that one over," Jack said.

"Well, thanks for telling me anyway," Grace said, her respect for him growing. Her mind went back to Maudie in *Mockingbird* saying some people were sent here to do our unpleasant jobs. Was Jack one of these people?

"Talk to you later," Jack said.

The phone went silent in her hand. Lindsey? Now she really felt like a dork. Here she'd been so upset that she might be hurting her when her so-called friend had been the one behind the vicious poster and note.

Grace let out a shriek, hopped off the bed, and ran to the door, shouting for Essence. Now she really needed the perfect outfit. For a moment clothes were more important than posters. "After all," she said out loud, "I am still a kid."

THOSE PEOPLE
US

At first Essence had said she wouldn't go to the dance, but then so many people had talked to her and assured her she ought to go that she had decided to go. Sister had been especially kind to her, inviting her into her office and telling her she would stick by her all through the dance just like glue. So here she was waiting to get into the car and go. Grace was so excited to be going to the dance with Jack. She had taken hours at the mall, trying on every top in Nordstrom's before she settled on a deep green blouse that made her eyes sparkle. Essence had made her choice first—a light blue top and black slacks—and then just sat while Grace picked over piles of clothes. Her mom's face had reddened with impatience again, her cheeks blushing and her toes tapping. She hoped each time the sales lady appeared with another top, rapping on the fitting room door, that this would be the one. The pile grew, a mound of as many shades of green as a forest housed. The thought of her daughter's first date with Jack gave her new patience.

"Come on, Gracie," her dad called. "Enough time in front of the mirror. You'll miss the dance."

Grace ran down the stairs and into the kitchen where her mom and dad were waiting, excited over their little girl's first dance with a boy. "Oh, you look great," her mom said, her eyes filling.

"Oh, please, Mom, don't cry," Grace warned, hearing her mother's voice wavering.

"Grace, isn't that a zit on your chin?" her dad said, pointing.

"What?" Grace shouted, aghast.

"He's just joking." Essence laughed. "You look fine."

"Sorry," her dad said. "Just trying to lighten everybody up. You look beautiful."

"You'd think a psychiatrist would know better than to be so cruel to his daughter," Grace laughed, touching her chin.

"She sure is beautiful," said Mrs. Beaudrie who was babysitting Char that night, "and Essence, that blouse is just gorgeous on you. Come on, Char, let's go upstairs and find us a movie to watch. No violence, you know I can't stand no blood. You all have a good time," she said with a flourish, taking Char by the hand.

"How about *The Lion King*?" Char asked.

"You're on," Mrs. Beaudrie laughed.

"Come on, girls," Mrs. Woodson cautioned. "Let's not be late."

Grace hadn't even objected when her parents had volunteered to be chaperones for the dance. She knew her dad would be calm if anything happened. She also was aware that Jack had decided to tell Sister Joan about the incidents and who was behind them Monday after the dance. Jack's dad was a chaperone, too. They would meet them in the school parking lot.

The girls ran out to the car and climbed into the back seat, waving goodbye to Idol who had crawled up on the foyer windowsill where she loved to sit on guard while everyone was away.

"One thing's for sure," Essence said. "Not much chance of Satchmo music tonight."

"Probably no Carrie tunes, either," sighed Grace.

"You two," said Mrs. Woodson from the front seat, chuckling and shaking her head.

"Maybe a Texas two-step," her dad added.

"Or a Cajun jig," said Essence.

They rode along the road to the school, their hearts light.

***

Across town guests were arriving at an elegant cocktail party given by the Townsends. Car after car deposited the elite of St. Cat parents. Two by two they entered into the marble foyer where a maid in a starched uniform took their light wraps. Lindsey had left for the dance already, riding with her friend, Madison. Her stepmother had gone on about what a shame it was she had no date, embarrassing her. The parents gathered in the salon, lit by a startling crystal chandelier. Tonight was a time to relax and enjoy the easy camaraderie of the suburban life they loved. A servant circulated with a tray of martinis, and a buffet offered a tantalizing display of dishes, catered by the finest firm in town. Mr. and Mrs. Townsend—the new super wife—mingled with their guests, happy to see how many people had accepted their invitation.

***

Grace was amazed. No one could have guessed that a few hours earlier sweaty boys had been doing laps around this gym, stopping to do push-ups for Coach. Now the room was a swirl of tiny lights, giggling girls, and handsome guys dressed in the latest in fashion. A few brave souls danced in the center of the floor beneath a huge silvery disco ball suspended from the rafters. A local band of tattooed guys rocked out, their hair almost long enough to cover most of their weathered, holey jeans. A group of girls hovered to the side near the drummer as he beat his sticks hard, rotating among the drums in a wild solo. A second cluster of girls stood up front near the lead singer, hanging on every note, moving with the lyrics, their eyes closed in some sort of dream state. Near the gym doors, a buzz went up as Jack and Grace walked in together. True to her word, Sister Joan, spotting Essence, came over to greet her.

"Well, I'm so glad to see you all tonight," Sister said with a big grin on her face.

***

"We're so happy that you've come," the new Mrs. Townsend sighed to the Johnsons. *He was a doctor and his wife an interior decorator. Mrs. Townsend, the first, did quite a bit of complaining to her daughter that all of HER friends had deserted her after the messy divorce. Now she was alone and NEVER asked to parties. It was hard enough for her to show up for school events, everyone staring, gossiping.*

"We wouldn't have missed it," Mrs. Johnson replied, sipping her martini, her persimmon lipstick staining the rim of the crystal. "And you look trés belle in that incredible dress. Who are you wearing, as they say on the red carpet?"

"Dior vintage," she said, smoothing the green taffeta skirt, hoping her hair looked fine, too. She'd spent most of the afternoon, having it highlighted.

"Ouch!" Mr. Johnson laughed. "No, we wouldn't have missed this party."

***

"We wouldn't have missed this dance," said Jack's father, Chuck Lowe, to Sister Joan. Grace knew he was a legend in the community. He was a top executive with the NASA space program, but seldom missed a school event for any of his four children. A more than generous supporter of all the teachers, he was always there when he was needed. Grace looked back and forth at Jack, then his dad. The same blue eyes stared out earnestly from beneath curly hair—Jack's brown, his dad's gray. Grace thought she and Jack looked good together. They were a lopsided match physically, she a full head shorter than he, but an even match in values.

The Woodsons and Mr. Lowe were soon deep in conversation with Sister so Jack, Grace, and Essence headed towards the dance floor. Coming towards them, they saw Sofia, her clothes a marked improvement on her erratically hemmed uniform. The four had taken a solemn pledge not to tell anyone they would be going to the dance together so now they had arrived like a southern storm with no warning at all. Heads turned, eyes popped, and mouths dropped as they made their way across the gym. Essence saw from the corner of her eye the group of girls standing by the drummer. Lindsey was the eye of that little storm.

***

The Booths walked across the plush taupe carpet and joined the conversation. The women were a gorgeous trio of red, black and green rustling dresses; the men in tuxes, penguin-like. Mr. Booth was a partner in the Townsend law firm, Mrs. Booth a charity volunteer.

"And what is new with the refugee situation?" Mr. Booth asked.

"I understand there was an incident with a poster in a locker," Mrs. Johnson added, sipping on her drink while she mentally assessed the value of the necklace Mrs. Booth was wearing. The girl could use a bit of Botox, she thought. Right between her eyes. And that red hair is just not making it.

Just then the servant passed by again, stiff in his uniform, and Mr. Townsend pulled him over, taking another drink from his tray. "Keep circulating, boy," he said. "Our guests are very thirsty tonight."

"Yes, sir." With a nod, the young man was off to re-fill his tray.

"Sister Joan overreacted as usual," Mrs. Townsend said, "Burning the poster in the chapel was ridiculous. It was just a harmless prank."

***

One of the girls looked over at the four newcomers to the dance and turned back to Lindsey, grabbing her shoulder and spinning her around. The words that emerged from her mouth would have gotten her a detention had any adult heard them, but they were softened to a mime by the constant drumming. Sofia read her lips however, and knew trouble would be arriving soon. Fear crept into her stomach as she followed behind Jack and Grace. Had they seen Lindsey? If they had, they were unfazed as they moved to the dance floor and began to dance. They looked good together as if they'd had a lot of practice. Yes, they were a good fit. Jack

NOLA Gals/Barbara J. Rebbeck

leaned slightly into Grace's wake as she spun around, her back to him.

Essence and Sofia stood alone, hoping to vanish into the wall. It was getting hard to breathe. Essence needed air. Walking quickly to the door, she was aware of Lindsey moving up behind her with Madison and Emily. Panicked and leaving Sofia behind, she ran back down the hall to the garden. Pushing the door open, she headed to the statue of Saint Catherine and dropped to her knees, closing her eyes, terrified. It was dark, the garden dimly lit by light streaming out from the windows along the hallway.

"I'm not a Catholic, but please help me," she prayed.

***

"Yes, Sister Joan did overreact. But she's always been a bleeding liberal," Mr. Johnson added. "I don't know why the Board ever hired her in the first place."

"Maybe we should suggest they look into her contract. Just because she's a nun doesn't mean she's untouchable," Mr. Booth suggested.

"This whole New Orleans business...these strange girls..." Mr. Townsend said, putting his arm around his wife.

"Now, honey, don't sound like a southern bigot. As long as they keep their distance and don't really mix in with our girls."

"You know they call themselves 'gals.' That New Orleans is as corrupt as the day is long. Some say Katrina was a fitting punishment for their sins," Mrs. Booth said, stroking her husband's arm.

"I thought the Woodsons had more sense than to take those girls in. I hope they are checking to see if the little brats have stolen them blind yet," Mrs. Johnson hissed, pushing a lock of hair from her husband's eyes.

"I understand there is real trouble with the refugees at the public high school. Gang fights, suspensions, theft," Mr. Townsend added, noticing Mrs. Booth's curves in her bright red dress, set off by her flaming auburn hair.

"How about some food?" Mrs. Townsend asked, sweeping her arm towards the buffet. "Come on, y'all. Chow's on!"

***

"You'd better pray," hissed Lindsey suddenly kneeling beside her in front of the statue. Madison dropped to her knees on the other side, while Emily stood behind her. Essence was trapped.

"Go home," said Madison.

"Go home," echoed Emily.

"Go home," the three chanted.

Essence shook herself free and jumped up, sobbing. "Leave me alone. Leave me alone." She backed up to the statue, falling backwards into the outstretched arms of Saint Catherine, shouting, "What have I done to you? Why do you hate me?"

"Girls!"

The three girls snapped back around to see Sister Joan, Jack, and Grace standing in the hallway door. "Get in this building NOW."

They froze, unable to move as Essence began to moan, sinking again to the ground, her arms above her head as she swayed back and forth.

Speaking to no one, but everyone, she questioned:

"Why has this happened to me?

Was I that bad?

Could I have been a better child?

Lord, wasn't I a grateful enough girl?

Didn't I love my Mimmi enough?

Was I too sassy?

Oh, Lord, help me. First you sent Katrina. Then Rita.

Oh, Saint Catherine, save me from these wicked girls.

I'll be better. I'll help. I'll pray."

***

As the couples passed down the buffet table, filling their plates with the delicious entrees, the men heaping plates much higher than their wives, the conversation continued.

"You know there are black students at Saint Cat's already," Mrs. Townsend said. "I saw a couple the last time I was there for a bake sale."

"Oh, yes, but you can't compare them to those NOLA kids. Their dads are all professional. They almost belong. At least they can pay the tuition," argued Mrs. Johnson.

"And thank God, you ladies do the bake sales so we daddies can earn a living," laughed Mr. Booth.

"I believe I earn a living, too," said Mrs. Booth, her plate holding a spear of broccoli and a single mushroom hors d'oeuvre. "Have to watch my waistline so I don't end up like the late Mrs. Townsend, the first," she said to no one in particular.

The three ladies stood together while their husbands branched out into the small crowd, no doubt networking for business contacts. "I saw the most peculiar sight," Mrs. Townsend said," I was cleaning up after the bake sale. Everybody else was gone for the day. I walked by the courtyard and saw Sister Joan and that little Char kid—you know, the one who can't spell her name correctly. I mean it's 'Chardonnay,' honey, with a big ol' 'Y!'"

"What were they doing? Praying?" asked Mrs. Johnson, nibbling a caviar concoction from her plate.

"No. Sister Joan was standing behind her while Chardonnai was sprinkling something around in front of the statue, crying her eyes out and shaking so bad I thought she'd fall over into the dirt. Some old black man was playing the trumpet. Ridiculous."

"Goodness. What next?" asked Mrs. Booth, eying another small group of women as if planning an escape.

"We need to take our school back. And have you read any of that ridiculous novel they're all reading? To Kill a Mockingbird? Obscene," Mrs. Townsend said, "A black man rapes a white girl. Can you believe our girls are reading that trash? Never you fear, I'm taking care of that. Wait for tomorrow's newspaper. You'll see. Now where is that boy with the drinks?"

***

By now Sister Joan, Jack, and Grace were by her side, but Essence remained on the ground, pushing them away. Sofia stood crying, afraid to approach.

"No," Essence whimpered, "I am bad. Lindsey is right."

"Essence, stop this. You are a good person. You have done nothing wrong," Sister continued, down on her knees, trying to gather Essence in her arms.

By now many more people had gathered. They lined the hallway, peering out into the courtyard from the windows in silence. A few of the New Orleans kids had begun to slowly form a circle around the statue and Essence, as if to spread a protective net around their friend.

"I dream every night that I am in the water again. That George is trying to pull me to the boat. That Mimmi is sinking below the water. That Mama is lost, crying for me to find her."

"Shhh," Sister whispered, again reaching for Essence.

Pulling against her, Essence said softly, "Do you think it's easy for me to get up every day and come to this school? Nothing makes this pain go away. Nothing."

Essence remained crumpled on the ground, her breath in hiccupped sobs, and her head in her hands. Grace and Jack stood back, shocked. Sister blocked her from Lindsey, Madison, and Emily who still stood frozen in place. Sofia stepped forward, dropping to the ground next to Sister, holding out her hand to Essence.

Then through the evening air, seeping gently as sweet molasses dripped the slow, soft notes of a trumpet. The lazy river. Essence lifted her head as the little protective group backed up a bit so she could see the trumpet man approaching as if an angel was coming to carry her home.

"Daddy?" she called out into the dark.

The trumpet answered for him, continuing its soft melody, soothing her heart.

GRACE

"It's called PTSD or Post-Traumatic Stress Disorder," Grace's dad said, explaining Essence's breakdown at the dance the night before. "Often after such a shock like Hurricane Katrina, survivors break down and relive it. Their minds take them right back to the ugly memories as if they are really there again. They relive the original trauma over and over again. I sent Mr. Lowe to bring Harold to the school when I saw what pain she was in. I thought he could help her—her music man."

Dr. Woodson had driven Harold and Essence back to his apartment when Essence had calmed down; and after talking to them both for a while, he had been assured she would be better off with her dad for the night. She had called Grace earlier this morning and said she felt much better, but too embarrassed to go back to school ever.

Char sat with them at breakfast, eating her favorite Cheerios. Grace didn't have much appetite, pushing her fruit around her plate, her mind on other things.

"Well, that was certainly a first date for you and Jack to remember always," said her mom, trying not to show too much concern.

"Maybe we should get out of town for a while, a little break," her dad suggested.

"Look at this," her mom said, pushing an internet article across to Grace.

She looked down to see a poor pooch, gazing up at her from the page, huge eyes begging. What was this about?

"There's an organization called Best Friends Animal Society which has set up a shelter in Tylertown, Mississippi. They are sending people into New Orleans to rescue animals and bring them back to them for treatment and adoption. They are asking for help, and I thought you and I might go."

"But I couldn't miss school…"

"I already checked with Sister Joan, and she thinks it's a great cause. She has approved your going if you keep a journal of your time there."

Grace realized this was already a done deal, and her mom was breaking it to her gently. "And Essence?"

"She'll be fine with her dad for now," her mom continued, taking the article back, "and she has Sofia."

"Dad?"

Her dad came out from behind the local newspaper long enough to weigh in on the notion. "Sounds like a great idea. It would get your mind off school for a time, plus you'd be doing so many good deeds, you'd be a sure bet for Heaven."

"I don't know," said Grace. "These poor animals must be so pathetic and sad. How long would we be gone?"

"Probably about two weeks," her mom replied. "It's about a six-hour drive. We'd use the van from my practice."

"Jack might want to go," her dad said.

"You're joking, right?" asked Grace, not quite believing her ears. She reached for her milk, looking over at Char who was quietly arranging her Cheerios along the rim of the bowl, oblivious to the conversation.

NOLA Gals/Barbara J. Rebbeck

"Mr. Lowe and I did discuss it. He thinks you're a good influence on Jack. And you would have many, many, many chaperones," her dad laughed. "Of course he'd want to be back for the play-offs. I can't believe it, but it appears the Astros are going to make it to the series."

"I can just hear the kids at school if he goes. Holy horrors!" Grace said, chugging her milk and licking her lips.

"We'll think about it. I want to leave Sunday," her mom finished, getting up to carry her empty plate into the kitchen. Her dad followed, leaving the newspaper on the table. Grace read the headline upside down, then swung the paper around to be sure she had read correctly: **Parents Challenge Mockingbird**. Beneath the headline was a photo of Lindsey's stepmom and the quote, 'This dangerous book must go! Our girls cannot read this filth.'

Looking over at Char, Grace said, "No wonder they want me out of town."

"You going away?" Char asked. "Hurry home. I love you."

She thought about the discussion they had had in Ms. Rodger's advisee group a few days ago about Banned Book Week. She'd been dismayed to find out that her all-time favorite novel, *To Kill a Mockingbird* was number thirty-one on the banned book list although it was read in about seventy-five percent of schools in the country. Lindsey had seemed very interested in the statistics, asking Ms. Rodgers to repeat them so she could write them down. Now she knew why Lindsey had looked up from discussing her latest nail polish shade with Madison. Now she knew. She re-read the article, shaking her head. *Poor Sister Joan*, she thought. *She doesn't deserve this new storm. Miss Harper Lee, they're coming for you.*

ESSENCE Journal
October 1, 2005

I feel better now. I am living with my daddy and Mrs. Beaudrie, and Char has just moved in today. I also have my good friend Sofia. She knows exactly what I'm going through. I spend a lot of time talking with Dr. Woodson about all my sorrows. He is so kind and knows just how I am feeling. He has talked to Char, too. She's too little to keep a journal so he's got her making a book of drawings. This morning she drew a heart that was split in two. On one side was Mimmi, and on the other was Mama. It reminded me of that ugly heart with the knife through it on the poster in my locker. I told her she should draw another heart showing what she still has. Not just what she's lost. So she's back at the table now coloring hard.

We haven't been back to school since the dance. I don't want girls laughing at me on account of how sad I got in the garden. I couldn't help it. When those evil girls came around me, I felt like the Devil himself was touching me, whispering for me to go home. All I could think of was my smashed up life, blown away by Katrina. And then just when I was trying to stand back up, Rita did her best to knock me down again. All my sadness came pouring out of me like my heart had broken, not just the levee. I'm so glad my daddy came to get me with his sweet music. That calmed me down so much I fell asleep on the ride home and slept most of the next day after Dr. Woodson talked to me. Sister says to take a little vacation and to settle into my new home, and then think about going back to school. She gave me the movie of To Kill a Mockingbird to watch while I'm home.

Home. This apartment will do for now. Char and I share a bedroom again. Daddy says we can paint the walls with whatever colors and pictures we want. That is our next project he says. We're going to go buy paint later. The landlord here says he'll pay for it. He's real nice to us because of all we lost from Katrina. Some folks do like us I guess.

I talk on the phone to Grace every day. She is going with her mom and her new boyfriend, Jack to a town in Mississippi to help rescue animals lost from the storms in New Orleans. I will miss her. She says they'll be gone two weeks and she will keep a journal so I can see what she was up to for all that time when she gets home. I pray every night that she will find silly old George floating around somewhere. I drew a picture of what he looks like so she can try to spot him.

Char has just given me her new drawing. It is a much bigger heart and she has drawn all these new friends we've made. Mrs. Beaudrie, Grace and her parents, Idol the cat, Jack and his dad, Sofia and her mom, Sister Joan, and of course, Harold. He's looking at the picture now, and just said that picture deserves a tune. He's taught Char to sing a sweet little song about hushing and not crying and papa buying her a mockingbird.

Papa, but where's Mama? Can't we have both?

Oh, the doorbell just rang and Sister was there. She had a whole bag of letters for Char and me. Lots of kids from schools all across the country have written to us. We were so happy that we dug into the bag and threw them into the air. It was raining letters. Sister laughed and threw more letters up. We all fell on the floor together almost like it was snowing letters like that time in Maycomb in

NOLA Gals/Barbara J. Rebbeck

Mockingbird when Jem made the snowman. Don't get snow here in Houston much. I love Sister. She hugged us both and said she had to get back to school. Now I have lots to read. And maybe I will write back, too. I do like to write. Ms. Rodgers says I am beginning to master the art of the comma.

GRACE
Journal
October 2, 2005

We're on the road to Tylertown. I promised Sister Joan and Ms. Rodgers that I would keep a journal, so here is my first entry.

We left early this morning to get a head start on the day. It was a warm day in Houston as we loaded the van, and we were all pretty excited to get on the road. We felt really great about being able to help all those displaced animals. As I write, I'm up front in the vet van with my mom, and Jack is snoozing in the back seat. I still can't believe that my parents and Jack's allowed him to come with us. Mom says traveling like this will be a good test of our friendship. Friendship? Okay, that's enough for now I guess. Before we left, Jack and his parents spoke to Sister about Lindsey, Madison, and Emily. We call them the three witches, but Mom says we're as bad as them when we do that. So they're suspended, and Lindsey's mom is hopping mad, threatening to pull all of her children out of school. Dad says she's channeling her anger and bigotry into a campaign to get To Kill a Mockingbird banned. And since she's married to a lawyer, she should know just how to attack. Mom promised me we will be back from Mississippi in time for the special hearing when Super Townsend makes her case. I really want to speak at the hearing, but I'm not sure they'll let me. After all, I'm only a kid. Dad says he'll monitor the Astros while we're gone and get tickets for the championship series if they win. That made Jack happy.

As I look out the window, the freeway seems to stretch out forever before us. The trip in total should take about six hours. We're on I-10 East now, and should stop for a snack soon. I'm starving. The bridge collapsed on this freeway in New Orleans, but we go north before that.

Before we left, Mom showed me an email from the Tylertown group about volunteering. They said to expect our stay to be like an "extreme camping" environment. So we'll be roughing it in a tent and sleeping bags. There is running water, but no access to showers or bathrooms. Porta-johns and stringy hair seem to be my future for the next two weeks. They say that cell phones work as well as laptops. In fact, one of the volunteer tasks is to load data into the computer network. Once pets are brought to the shelter, all the info about each one such as where it was found and a complete physical description are recorded. This info is matched with missing pet reports with hopefully a reunion in sight.

Jack's awake. At least he doesn't snore. He's really kind of cute—just leaned forward and touched my nose, saying he was glad he came. He's going to get the chance to see the real me. My blow dryer is left behind in Houston. Make-up, too. We're looking for an exit with food signs. I could do a Big Mac about now, but I have to remain true to Carrie and be a veggie so I'll let Mom and Jack go for the Big Macs. I'll settle for a salad. So that's it for now, Sister Joan. No heavy life lessons yet. But I'm sure there will be many along the way. Stay tuned.

ESSENCE, DEAR FRIEND

Dear New Friend,

I'm so sorry the hurricane wrecked your home and life. I hope you have dried out and not lost too much stuff. I am sending you a dollar to buy candy. That should make you happy.

Love, Brandy, Grade 3

Dear Survivor,

I hope you are safe now. I will pray for you every night. God will drive the devil out of New Orleans. Can you send me some Mardi Gras beads?

Kisses, Jane, Grade 3

Barbara J. Rebbeck/NOLA Gals

Dear Boy or Girl,

I was sad when I heard about that bad storm. Were you scared? They said on TV it sounded like a train coming. I hope you find a new place to live. Here is a baseball card from the Detroit Tigers for you to keep.

Bye Bye, Joey, Grade 3

Dear Survivor,

That's a scary word to be called. Did you lose your pet? I hope not. Here is a photo of my cat, Precious. Do you like her? You can't have her, just look at her picture.

Love, Jackie, Grade 3

Dear Friend,

I am an eighth grader at Abraham Lincoln Middle School in Michigan. When I saw all the damage to your city on TV, I wanted to know what I could do to help you. My teacher suggested we all write letters to you. But that was not enough for me so my mom and I sent money to The Red Cross. I don't know if you will get any of it, but I hope so.

I am 13 years old and love school. I am on the soccer team and love to dance, too. Where are you going to school now? I heard all the schools in New Orleans are a mess. I hope you found a new school that you like as much as your old one. We are having our first dance this week with a DJ. I don't have a boyfriend yet, but have my eye on Jacob who is sooooo cute.

Well, that's all for now. Please write back.

Love, Ellen, Grade 8

NOLA Gals/Barbara J. Rebbeck

Dear Friend,

My name is Joseph, and I am in the 8th grade. I was horrified to watch the storm hit your city. I have been to New Orleans for Mardi Gras and loved it because when we left my own city in February to go there, we had snowdrifts all around. Have you ever seen snow? It's cool at first, but when April comes around, and the snow keeps coming it gets really aggravating. Besides, my dad makes me shovel it all. So life in Minnesota can be tough. I hope the government gets its act together to give you more help. We are sending these letters to Houston so I know you must be living there somewhere. I hope your family has survived. It would be very hard to lose a member to a hurricane. And I hope your pets are okay, too. They all look so sad on CNN. I saw one poor dog stranded on top of a car that was half-covered with water.

Our teacher said to send you something from Minnesota so I am enclosing one of the first fall leaves I have seen from a big oak not far from our school. I hope you will get home soon and be able to march in the Mardi Gras parade next winter.

That's all for now, Joseph, Grade 8

Dear Friend,

My name is Tom, and I am learning to play the trumpet. Have you heard of Louis Armstrong? Do you know the song about missing New Orleans? I take private lessons and my teacher helped me record my version of this song for you. It is enclosed for you. I hope you like it. We worked hard on it. I'm lucky to live in a safe city that doesn't get hurricanes or tornadoes ever. Good luck to you in the future. I am black, and think the government should be doing more for you. What do you think?

Tom, Grade, 9

***

Essence put her head down on the table, exhausted yet uplifted by her reading. A mound of letters still sat on the floor in the bag by her, but she stacked the open ones to her left, and then made another little pile of gifts in front of her. A photo of a black spotted cat. A baseball card of Al Kaline. A dollar to buy candy. A golden oak leaf. A CD of a sad song about missing New Orleans. *Thank you, Boo Radley*, she thought. Many kids across the country did love this New Orleans ghost of a gal. *Ils aiment.*

She pulled back the covers on her bed and looked over at little Char, sleeping the sleep of angels. But she decided to try one more letter first. The letters helped her so much, almost holding her like a blanket, making her feel warm. Walking back to the desk, she dug her hand in the bag and drew out one more. She looked at the envelope and almost dropped it when she saw her name scrawled across it. Who knew her name?

Essence,

I hope this letter gets to you somehow and that you are okay and safe. It's your old neighbor, Billy writing to you. Me and my family are in Mississippi staying with my mama's family. Where are you? We are all safe and no one was hurt, but we sure got soaked along the way. Mississippi (I just learned to spell that word right!) got hurt bad, too. But we are doing fine. I don't know if we will ever get back to New Orleans. I heard the houses in our ward are all drowned. I hope you guys all escaped. Mimmi was so stubborn. Is George okay? I miss tossing the ball for him. Mama said I should try to get this letter to you. You never know, she said. I miss you.

Billy

No, you never know, Essence thought, as tears rolled down her cheeks.

GRACE

After the McDonald's break, they had sailed along the freeway, arguing about what music to play. Not wanting to risk their first fight, Jack had finally given in to listening to Carrie Underwood for a while, only after being assured he had next choice.

"In this family, you had better learn to love or at least tolerate Carrie," Grace's mom had warned him. As Grace sang along in the front seat, Jack quietly turned his iPod on, turning his head, pretending to fall asleep again. Mrs. Woodson smiled as she looked in the rear view mirror and saw exactly what Jack was doing. *Smart boy*, she thought.

It had been a rough week and she was happy to be on the road, able to get Grace out of town before Mrs. Townsend's new storm broke. Book burning was something new for the school. Sister Joan was horrified, but with her hands tied, had to agree to fight it out at a formal hearing. "Surely," she had told the

Woodsons and Lowes, "the parents in this community are more enlightened than this. The book was written forty-five years ago."

Ms. Rodgers, Grace's favorite teacher, had been given the formidable task of defending her reading choice, knowing that as Tom Robinson had lost his case in the novel—even though he was obviously innocent of the crime--she too might well be toppled by the likes of Mrs. Townsend and her group of supporters—loud among them the Johnsons and Booths. As Ms. Rodgers was a teacher and woman of integrity, Grace's mother knew she would resign if the fight was lost and the novel banned.

"Look at him, Mom," Grace said, "Asleep again."

"The sleep of angels," Mom sighed.

"Hardly. No, I'm awake." Jack said, sitting up. "Just resting my eyes."

Both women laughed out loud at this excuse. They had heard it many, many times before from Grace's dad.

"Mom, how about a bathroom break? That diet coke—right on through me."

"Next exit, Grace."

Jack leaned forward and tapped Grace on the shoulder. She turned and looked into his blue eyes and felt a little flutter in her stomach. He loomed large in her gaze, his old blue t-shirt the perfect color for accentuating those eyes. Sister had suggested they wear their St. Cat's school shirts as representatives of the community. They had packed them, but opted for old, comfy clothes for the long ride.

"Yes?" Grace asked, locking eyes with him and smiling her best.

"I'm glad I came," he said, grinning and touching the tip of her nose. "That's all," he said, leaning back in the seat.

Grace looked over at her mom and rolled her eyes, her heart thumping against her old oversized shirt.

"Nice," her mom mouthed to her, hoping Jack hadn't seen. *Sister is not going to read about a lot of this trip,* she thought. *Not in Grace's journal, anyway.*

"Exit," Jack called from the back, pointing right.

"Yes, sir."

NOLA Gals/Barbara J. Rebbeck

Jack and Mrs. Woodson leaned against the side of the van just in front of the *Woodson Veterinary Practice on Wheels* lettering, making small talk waiting for Grace. Jack kicked the loose gravel with his foot, head down, breaking a sweat in the hot sun.

Grace ran up to them, biting into an ice cream bar—her favorite, chocolate sundae.

"None for us?" Jack asked, squinting into the sun behind Grace. They had stopped at a pretty rundown gas station. Jack had pumped gas for the ladies as they headed to the bathroom, and then stayed with Mrs. Woodson as Grace shopped in the small store.

"No, nothing at all," she replied, laughing as she handed over candy bars for both of them. "I know, I know. Not healthy at all, but I figure we'd better have a sugar high because who knows what hardships lie ahead of us."

"Let's hit the road," Mrs. Woodson said. "We should be in Tylertown by early afternoon."

Jack helped Grace back up into the front seat of the van, closed the door, and then slid the back door open.

"He thinks I'm made of glass," Grace mumbled to her mom, clicking her seat belt on and smiling.

"Oh, it's sweet, honey," her mom replied, belting up, too. "Save your energy for what's ahead."

Jack, secured in the backseat, asked, "So what jobs do you think they'll have us do?"

"Data entry is one," Grace replied, turning her head to look at Jack. She had thought about sitting back there with him for the last leg of the trip, but didn't want to chance aggravating her mom. Better to wait till it was her mom's idea.

"And if you want to get your hands—and arms—and whole body dirty and wet, there's always dog washing," Mrs. Woodson said, watching in the mirror for Jack's reaction.

"That's for me," said Jack, smiling back into the mirror.

"The two of you might be a good pair for that job," Mrs. Woodson said. "Jack, do you have any pets?"

"Yes," he said. "Two Labs. Shep and Gus."

"Where'd you come up with those names?" Grace asked.

"They were two of the original Mercury astronauts. Alan Shepard and Gus Grissom," Jack answered. "Dad started reading me bedtime stories about them when I was just a little kid. It was a fast move from *Goodnight Moon* to space walks."

"Oh, yes," Mrs. Woodson said, "I'd forgotten about your dad's NASA connections."

"Actually, I'm named after one of my dad's heroes, Astronaut Jack Lousma. He and my dad were both born in Michigan. I'm hoping I'll be in space someday. In the Mars program."

"Why didn't your dad join the program?" asked Mrs. Woodson.

"Bad eyes. He knew he'd never pass so he went for engineering."

"It's obvious he loves what he's doing, on the ground or in the air," Mrs. Woodson continued, remembering an enlivened conversation just the other night at the dance.

"What about you, Grace?" Jack asked. "Ever thought of flying? I know you're a brainiac."

"Not sure what I want to do," Grace said, a bit intimidated by Jack's future plans. "Maybe a lawyer."

"Enough of the future," Mrs. Woodson said, sliding a CD into the player. "Time for some jazz."

Groaning as the first sounds of jazz filled the air, both Jack and Grace plugged their iPods into their ears and eased back in their seats, intent on enjoying their last leisurely moments for a long time. "Jazz never ends," said Grace, sighing. It just goes on, and on, and on. Not like my Carrie."

"Give me Miles Davis anytime," said Mrs. Woodson.

ESSENCE
Letters
October 5, 2005

Dear Tom,

When Sister brought me a big bag of letters from kids across the USA, I was so happy. I set out to answer every one of them, but now I realize I can't do that. It would take forever so I am picking just some to answer. Yours is one. I loved your trumpet playing, and yes I know that song. It is very sad for me to listen to now because of how much I do miss New Orleans. When I see the photos on TV, it makes me cry. It seems to me like The Big Easy was like a giant bowl that filled up with everybody's tears. Some good things came out of Katrina. I found my daddy, Harold at the Dome when we were stranded there. It was pretty bad. Man, did it stink. Too many souls stuck there for too long. But I had not seen my daddy for a long time. Then I found out he was there and had been living in the 7th Ward all along, but I was living in the 9th Ward with my Mimmi and Mama and sister, Char. (That's short for Chardonnai.) My daddy plays the trumpet, too, and when he listened to your music, he said you played just fine for a boy your age. My Mimmi died after the storm. She made Char and me get in the boat that came to rescue us at our old house. My mama was missing. When we got to the Astrodome we met the two Dr. Woodsons. They are married and he takes care of people's mental problems while she takes care of pets. Anyways, they have a daughter named Grace who has been very good to me. My sister and me came to live with them, and Harold and his friend, Mrs. Beaudrie got an apartment. I think Grace's dad must be paying the rent for them because the government isn't doing so hot helping us all. It takes too long for everything. Is it because we're black? Maybe. I just read a book called, To Kill a Mockingbird. Have you read it? It tells how a black man named Tom Robinson was found guilty of a crime even though he didn't do it. It took place in Maycomb, Alabama in 1932. He had a good lawyer named Atticus, but he lost anyway. His

NOLA Gals/Barbara J. Rebbeck

daughter was a lot like my new friend, Grace. She didn't understand what was going on and why people were so mean. At the school I'm going to now in Houston, there are really nice people like Sister Joan and Ms. Rodgers, the one who had kids read Mockingbird, but there are also some real mean girls who tell me to go home all the time and put bad posters in my locker. I don't know what I have done wrong. I got real sad at a dance they had and now I have moved in with my daddy. Then yesterday a big surprise happened. The doorbell rang and there was Dr. Woodson and my mama. I was so happy I jumped into her arms. Seems after Katrina she had been sent all the way to Kansas on an airplane, and The Red Cross had finally found her and hooked us up. I thought it would be great with the whole family back together until Dr. Woodson left and Mama and Daddy started fighting real bad. I cried and yelled at them to stop yelling and cursing at each other. Mama said we were going to go live with her because she would not let her girls stay with Harold and his woman, Mrs. Beaudrie. I was sad because I liked Mrs. Beaudrie a lot, and she has been like a mama to Char and me. But that's what Mama didn't like at all. So Mama stomped off, saying she'd be back for us. Then Harold started talking crazy about how he'd just have to leave with us all and hide somewhere that Mama couldn't find us. Char started sobbing then, saying she hated

Mama for ruining everything. So just when it seemed like there were some happy things in my life again, it seems that hurricane blew us all away again in all different directions. I wish Mimmi was here to hold me. I feel alone again. Grace and her mama have gone to Mississippi to help rescue pets. I miss talking to them, and I hope Harold doesn't hide us before they get home. I always had a dream that Harold would find me and play his sweet music and then we'd all be a family again, but it doesn't look like that at all for now.

Well, Tom I'm sorry to go on about my troubles. I guess I just need someone to talk to. Maybe I'll answer more letters. Please write back.

Your new friend, Essence

Dear Joseph,

It must be very cold in Minnesota. I have never seen snow, but I have seen too much wind and rain. Way too much. We lost our dog George when they wouldn't put him in the rescue boat with us. Our grandma died too, but she was a hero who made me and my sister go ahead in the boat without her. A boy named Joey sent me this baseball card. It says on the back that Al Kaline is from Detroit. That must be near you where they get snow so I am sending the card to you for being so nice to write to me and send me the beautiful leaf. I have a new friend in Houston. Her name is

NOLA Gals/Barbara J. Rebbeck

Grace. Her mom is a vet and they are in Mississippi to help rescue pets. I hope they will find George.

Your new friend, Essence

Dear Billy,

I was never so surprised to find your letter in a big bag of letters I got from kids all across the U.S. of A. I'm not so good as you. Seems like you are one lucky kid. I am in Houston. Good thing is I found my daddy and yes, indeed like I suspected he is the man in that old photo I showed you. But the bad thing is we found Mama after she was sent to Kansas and she HATES my daddy. All they do is fight and curse. But the worst thing is Mimmi died in our white house when it flooded. Char and me were rescued by two men in a boat, but Mimmi stayed behind with George. And who knows where skinny George got himself to? I hope he's found himself some food and is keeping away from ladies' dainties. We have met some good folks here, but the girls at school mostly hate me and Char. It's a real fancy school with rich girls in hot, itchy uniforms. I have some friends named Grace and Sofia. I need to go to bed now. I will write again soon. My hand is tired with all this writing and it's hard to write about such sorrows. Char says hello. We miss you.

Essence

GRACE
Journal
October 3, 2005

Well, Sister, Tylertown is quite an experience. We arrived yesterday at the St. Francis Sanctuary, driving the final miles through areas just on the road back from the destruction, trees strewn about like plastic toys, mud everywhere ready to suck you in up to the ankles, electricity just poking back on in jolts. We registered at the front table and were put to work immediately after a short tour. Kind of chaotic, but they were so happy to see more help coming in.

It's really amazing and sad at the same time, what these people have been able to do so quickly under such poor circumstances. Jeff was our guide, a scruffy (that adjective pretty much describes everyone here) fortyish guy with a fresh beard and little half glasses hanging from a chain around his neck. He walked around with a clipboard, making checks

NOLA Gals/Barbara J. Rebbeck

now and then, more data destined for computers. They were so glad to see us, but particularly my mom. She will be doing intake exams of all the animals as they arrive.

Jeff pointed out to us that the area was divided into different locations: Toytown for the smaller dogs, Pooch Alley for the big ones, and three buildings for cats. Volunteers had been put to work building large dog runs that could hold up to 600 four-footed evacuees. He explained the dogs were too traumatized to be put into crates, that they needed the outdoors and the freedom to run about. The trucks were still arriving daily, filled with sad-eyed survivors, many with serious illnesses and injuries, the least of all malnutrition. The cats proved to be the hardest to rescue as they hid all over the place, afraid to come out into the muck of the receding water and stubborn as only felines can be, he said.

Walking alongside of Jeff, I felt here was another hero sent here to do an impossible job, and I was so happy I was here to help. I was useful.

To look into the eyes of these poor creatures is to understand their pain and trauma. Whoever made the rule that people had to abandon their pets to Katrina's aftermath should be here, walking through Toytown and Pooch Alley, hearing the whimpers and seeing the sores and wounds. Knowing how sad Essence and Char are and that they worry all the time about old George is bad enough, but to multiply their pain times all the animals here is horrifying. Surely, Sister, this haven is a heaven for these unsuspecting victims of that monstrous storm. I'll be sure to give extra hugs to all these lost pets just like the girls would grab George and never let him go again.

ESSENCE

"I want my girls, now," Mama yelled at Harold, swinging her purse at him, barely missing his head.

"But, Baby, where you gonna go with them?" Harold said, trying to calm her down, grabbing the purse as she swung it again, catching it in midair.

They faced off together in the entry to the small apartment, defying each other, Mama breathing hard, spitting fire from her magic eyes.

"Now look how upset you're getting yourself. You're heaving up and down about to have a fit," Harold continued.

"Shut your mouth," Mama yelled. "Who do you think you are? How many years you been gone, not caring a whit for these girls?" she said heatedly, waving her free arm at Essence and Char who cowered in the living room.

"But I was here for them when they lost Mimmi. And they thought you were gone, too. Where you been anyway? With one of your dancing men?"

"Better a dancing man than a music man," she said, wrestling her purse free. Calming herself, she pulled her flowered smock back into place, aware of the girls watching them.

"Now come sit down in the living room and we'll talk," said Harold, showing the way to a worn old couch.

"Where's that woman?" Mama asked, her eyes flashing, searching around her as she sat down, gesturing for the girls to come sit by her. "Come here, my babies. Come to your mama. Get away from that old man."

"I have told you and told you over and over again that Mrs. Beaudrie is just my friend. She's at work," Harold replied, sinking into a faded armchair across the small room. "Woman, must you always be so difficult?"

"I'll bet she's supporting you. How else could you afford this place?" she asked, hugging the girls to her.

Essence, hoping to restore peace, said, "Dr. Woodson helps with the rent."

"He seemed like a real good man when we talked on the way here," Mama said. "A real fine man, educated and all, not like this piece of tooting trash."

"That's right. He's a fine man," said Harold, "and he tried real hard to find you. And as for this 'piece of trash,' I'll have a paying gig real soon downtown to pay more rent."

Rolling her eyes, Mama said, "Now where have I heard those sorry, lying words before?"

"But Daddy plays so good," little Char said, leaning her head into her mama's chest, smiling over at Harold.

Harold looked back at Char, returning her smile, ready to go grab his trumpet and play them all a tune.

"Child," Mama said, turning Char's face back to her, "don't you let this man put his spell on you. That man never paid the rent," Mama said, shaking her head, recalling years of scraping together money for bills, years of having to leave Essence to Mimmi's care to make ends meet.

"But we never lost the house," Harold said, thoughts of the trumpet dying in his mind like Mama had always killed his dreams.

"What you saying, old man? That house was never yours. It was Mimmi's and mine."

"Don't matter now. That house is gone as sure as Katrina's left town," Harold continued.

"I've got a job," Mama said, "And I want the girls to come live with me."

"Where you working?" Harold asked, "And why is it you think you're the best for these girls?"

"I'm about to come over there and smack you a good one, old man. Why am I the best? Why am I the best? This man is as dangerous as a Louisiana gator, girls. Don't you trust him or he'll bite your head right off." Little Char burrowed further into her mama's arm, her eyes wide.

"Don't you turn them girls against me. Mrs. Beaudrie and me found them all alone at the Dome. Mimmi dumped them in some stranger's boat and sat with that old dog in her house till her heart gave out. We saved their butts."

"But you got no job. You living on white folk's charity and the government. Who knows if they'll ever come through? Me, I'm starting work at a nursing home not far from here. They're gonna let me live in a room there and bring the girls."

"You crazy, woman? You and these girls living in one room in an old folk's home?" Harold sputtered, worried now. "You've lost your mind. That's no place for raising kids. Smells like pee all the time. Enough to make you gag. And half of them old folks is crazy. Just not safe. May as well be living in a swamp full of gators."

"And you about to make me gag. What do you know about raising kids?" Mama yelled back, tears running down her face.

Alarmed, Essence started to cry softly, tears sliding down her cheeks. Where was her dream? Where was the balcony she'd sit on, listening to her daddy's music? Where was her family?

Mama got up, twisting away from the girls, pulling free. She crossed the room, her face teary, but resolved and leaned over Harold who was slumped in the chair. "Listen," she said, her voice rock solid, "you have no right to these girls. You left us. I put food on the table for years. I was there every night for them.

NOLA Gals/Barbara J. Rebbeck

Thank God for Mimmi and her house. At least she put a roof over our heads. Do you hear me?" She grabbed his chin, her eyes piercing his. His tears came now as he returned her glare, shaking. She backed up, dropping her hand from his face, gesturing for the girls to come to her side.

Essence and Char ran to her, their arms reaching round her hips from each side.

"I'm leaving you girls here tonight, but I'll be back tomorrow night after I get myself settled. You have your things packed. Do you understand? And no funny business from you, old man. You try to run with my girls and I'll track you down like the old tired, worn out ugly dog you are.

"Now babies, give me one more hug and some sloppy sweetness," Mama said, hugging them both as close as she could. And with that she was out the door.

***

Dear Ellen,

Thank you so much for writing to me. And thank you for giving money to The Red Cross for all of us hurt by Katrina and Rita. Yes, since you wrote to me Hurricane Rita hit bad again. But I am safe in Houston for now. My mama has been found in Kansas, and she is now in Houston so our family is together. She is fighting with my daddy now, but I am sure if I am good enough I can make it all better. They make me sad all over again. I will be the best gal ever, and then they will love each other and we can be a true family. You'll see.

We had a dance at school, too. The music was good, but not as good as jazz in New Orleans. I hope your dance was good and Jacob likes you. I have made two friends here. One is Grace from Houston; the other is Sofia from New Orleans. My little sister Char is here too. I don't have a boyfriend yet.

Your new friend,
Essence

GRACE

J ack pointed the hose at Grace, squirting her instead of the thin Cocker Spaniel crouching between them.

"Jack!" she yelled, laughing, leaning forward to jerk the hose from his hands.

"Oh, no you don't. You could use a good shower," Jack said.

The two volunteers were working, giving baths to new intakes after they'd been examined by the vets. This little spaniel—under the muck and oil—was turning out to be a tan color. He'd come in this morning, very weak, drained of fluids, a cut on his back. Grace's mom had started an IV and patched up the cut with a few stitches, and within a few hours, he had perked up enough for a bath and his first meal.

Jack, having refocused the hose on the dog, said to Grace, "What do we call this one?"

It seemed odd to be naming these dogs that obviously already had names at their ages; but unless they had a tag on, it was up to them to rename them.

"How about Buff?" replied Grace, assessing the poor little dog. The dog began barking as if in approval, so Jack lifted the hose onto the dog's forehead, saying "I name thee, Buff."

Just then Mrs. Woodson stuck her head out the doorway across the yard and yelled for them to take the dog over to Pooch Alley and come on back to talk to her. Even under these grimy circumstances, she still managed to look as professional as possible, her hair drawn back in a ponytail, her scrubs clean.

Jack leaned over and picked up Buff and the two of them set off to show him his new temporary home.

"Do you think they'd let us take a dog home?" Jack asked, holding out Buff at arm's length from his chest, hoping his jeans wouldn't soak through and through.

"I suppose so," said Grace. "We brought a couple of crates with us to get them home."

"I wonder what Lindsey is doing right now," Jack said. "Maybe planning one of her rainbow parties. Or a White Power Rally."

Grace blushed at the suggestion of such a forbidden party and kept on walking, her head down, preferring to talk about dogs and adoption.

"Last summer when you went out of town to visit your grandmother, Lindsey had quite the party," Jack said, looking over the wriggling spaniel at Grace, trying to make her look up.

"Yes, she told me," Grace replied, meeting Jack's eyes, hoping the color spreading across her cheeks wasn't noticeable to him.

"She said she didn't tell you the gory details because you were just too childish and Catholic to accept what went on. That you might tell your parents, or worse yet, Sister."

Blushing again, all Grace could say at her best friend's betrayal was, "Oh." Was this Jack's way of warning her about what he expected in a relationship? Maybe Lindsey was the right girl for him after all. What did he want with her?

They had arrived at the Alley. Dogs of different breeds, sizes and colors jumped and ran, yapping and pouncing, roughhousing

NOLA Gals/Barbara J. Rebbeck

with each other, glad to be free from the Orleans deadly soup. Jack went over to check Buff in officially and Grace stayed back, sitting down under a tree, uncomfortable. She knew many of the eighth grade girls had talked of parties that were a way of growing up sexually. She knew what a rainbow party was. How far had Jack gone? And Lindsey? Madison had even declared in Advisee one day before Ms. Rodgers arrived that it was her goal to give a guy a special birthday gift, the present of his life actually, before the year was out. Grace sat quietly in the Mississippi heat, wondering how many parties she'd not been invited to. And what Jack expected of her. She remembered one party at Lindsey's when couples had rotated two minutes in a dark closet. She'd been left out, having no partner at the time. Suddenly Lindsey's entire story about Jack bringing her roses at school seemed ridiculous. Banned from seeing each other at school, but huddling in dark closets at parties? How hypocritical. How stupid. And she thought how inexperienced she was. How useless.

"So, should we go back to your mom's?" Jack asked, walking over to the tree and plopping down beside her.

"I suppose so," Grace said, looking across to the dogs, watching Buff meet his runmates.

"Did I upset you about Lindsey's party?"

Looking at Jack, Grace felt the color rising in her cheeks again. "Not really, but I do feel kinda stupid, childish."

Jack leaned over and brushed her lips with his, then leaned back, his blue eyes on hers. "Not childish," he said. "But you could use a shower."

Jumping up, he pulled her to him and hugged her, their soggy clothes seeping water and suds like a kitchen sponge being squeezed. "Let's go," he said. "Gracie, we're going to have such stories to tell. You know I have to write poems about this for my English teacher. I have a confession to make. I actually do like to write poetry. Don't you dare tell anyone," he said laughing and grabbing Grace's hand.

"That's soooo childish," Grace laughed, feeling his hand cold from the water in hers.

Chatting easily as they walked back, Grace began to recover from the latest blow from her friend, Lindsey. Maybe it was time to stop calling her a friend at all. As they crossed the walkway, Grace's mom came out to see them, raising her hand to her eyes to block the late afternoon sun. She looked tired to Grace. They'd been here a week now, working all day, and then sleeping in their small tent every night in sleeping bags. The ground was hard, but they slept soundly.

Last night they had gathered around a campfire with several other volunteers and swapped rescue stories. They heard from the men and women who spent their days in the cities. They heard heartbreaking stories of dogs found guarding their dead owners who had refused to evacuate without them. They heard tales of persnickety cats who had to be baited to get them to the trucks. They heard accounts of dogs that refused to get into boats, but swam, leading the boat back to trapped victims. The tears flowed as they let out the stored pain of their rescue efforts. A week into this, Grace found it silly to talk about any parties, and she wondered if she would ever fit in again with her Houston friends. This was life. Tragedy and resilience. Life and death.

"Good news," said Grace's mom as they approached. "We've been invited to McComb, not too far from here. St. Andrew's Mission has power and water, and they want us to come for dinner and showers."

"Yes!" shouted Grace.

"Wow," said Jack. "What's for dinner?"

"Where's the shower?" laughed Grace, looking down at her soggy, wrinkled jeans.

Just then a local lady came up to them, smiling and laughing. Her t-shirt was wet and stained, her jeans frayed and sticking to her legs, but she seemed so full of energy. Her gray hair stuck to her forehead in slick curls as she all but bubbled over, saying, "Why, we got plenty of food for you all at the mission. Tonight is our big weekly meal. Food's being sent in from all over. Now that we have power and water, we'll be fixing a feast. Fried chicken, smoked sausage, sweet potato casserole, fried eggplant, cabbage, rice and gravy, and for dessert, bread pudding." She laughed,

NOLA Gals/Barbara J. Rebbeck

proud to offer her long list, her eyes weary, but spirited. "Our farms have been knocked out by the storms, but we're coming back just fine. Take's time is all. And we're so glad you all are here helping these poor animals."

"Sounds good. I think we can make it," Jack said jokingly, shaking hands with the lady. "I'm Jack."

"And I'm Mrs. Reed. And you must be Grace. Your mama is talking my ear off about you. She sure is proud. She says you're a vegetarian, but we can fix you up just fine."

Grace reached out, embarrassed, and shook her hand, saying, "That won't be a problem at all. Mrs. Reed, did Mom say you're from Maycomb?"

"No, honey, that's McComb, but I know what you're thinking. That *Mockingbird* book. Takes place in Maycomb. Lots of folks confuse us. I must read that book someday."

ESSENCE Journal
October 10, 2005

We are on the road. Scared as hell and real guilty that we are leaving Mama after we just found her again. But Harold says we are just kids and don't know better. Harold said no way would he let us go live in a nursing home. He said just wait until we smelled the place. He knew it would smell like pee he said cuz he had played at those places at Christmas time and Good Lord we were not going to live there. He looked at us hard and said Lord knows why but he loves us both and will protect us. So Mrs. Beaudrie called a friend of hers she met in Houston who was going back to New

NOLA Gals/Barbara J. Rebbeck

Orleans and he said we could ride with him. Daddy is sure he can get a job playing trumpet in the French Quarter. Mrs. Beaudrie's friend, Louis, says there are jobs cleaning up the mess in the hotels so they can open again.

So we're scrunched in this old van, all five of us. Louis seems nice. Mrs. Beaudrie says he is a good man. He's a little bit fat and breathes real hard, barely fits behind the wheel. He wears this funny looking beret, tilted on one side of his head with long locks down his neck. Daddy says he's a hell of a drummer, though. Sorry Sister, for the language, but that's exactly what Daddy said. I can't see Louis beating hard on drums though, seems he'd have a heart attack working so hard.

Daddy worked fast, and before Mama could come and get us, we were on the road. Mrs. Beaudrie packed us some fine chicken sandwiches that we just ate. Char is curled up asleep next to me in the middle seat. Mrs. Beaudrie is snoring on the other side of me while I try to see enough to write this. I'm using a flashlight Louis says is for emergencies, but he reckons my journal counts as one. Got to record the truth, he said. For a minute I thought it must be Mimmi talking to me again. So here is some truth for whoever reads this journal. I am scared. I am scared to be in this old van on the road to a city that Katrina did her best to wreck. I am scared of what we will find when we get there. I am scared that Mama will follow us somehow like a detective. I am scared of what will happen when she meets up with Harold again. I am scared. I feel like Scout and Jem walking alone in the dark, hearing scary sounds, just waiting for someone to jump out at them. I am really scared.

GRACE

It felt good to be clean again. The little celebration at the mission last night had been great. After Grace, her mom, and Jack had all showered, they had stuffed themselves with an incredible meal. Then they had all indulged in their new favorite pastime, storytelling. When there is no TV or computer, your own words take center stage. Sitting around the mission patio, they had told their best pet rescue stories, almost competing for who could get the tears rolling down cheeks fastest. But now, today, they were back at their volunteer jobs. Grace's mom was examining a new truckload of arrivals. Jack was bathing the newcomers and walking some of the veterans. Grace was on duty on the computers, typing intake data for each new pet. They would all meet up for lunch, a meager one compared to last night's feast, but still appreciated.

As Grace worked at her computer in the makeshift office, her cell phone began to sing a Carrie tune to her so she grabbed it.

"Hello," she said.

"Grace, this is Sister Joan. We have a small crisis here. Have you heard from Essence at all?"

"Oh, hi, Sister," Grace replied, "No, not for a few days. Why? What's up?"

"She seems to be missing. Her mother was just here, furious. It seems Harold, Mrs. Beaudrie, Essence, and Char have left the city with a man named Louis. At least that's what the landlord at the apartment said."

"You're kidding," Grace said, "How?"

"Apparently, Louis has an old van," Sister Joan said. Grace could hear the worry in her voice.

"Where are they headed?" Grace asked, trying to think where they might have gone.

"Their mom seems to think they may be headed back to New Orleans because Harold had talked about getting a job playing in one of the hotels in the French Quarter."

"Well, if I hear anything from her, I'll let you know," Grace volunteered. "I'm sure Harold will take good care of them. Please don't worry, Sister."

"Pray for those girls, Grace."

"I will, Sister."

"How's everything there?" Sister asked, trying to overcome her worry enough to chat.

"We're just fine," Grace said, playing Sister's game. "Today I'm typing data in while Jack bathes newcomers. Mom is examining the new arrivals. They still keep coming by the truckloads."

"Bless you for your work, Grace. Say hi to your mom and Jack. We're all praying for you."

"Thank you, Sister, but take your prayers for us and heap them on Essence," Grace laughed, trying to cheer her up.

"Grace, you've grown so much. You're one of Katrina's blessings. Got to run now; Sister Margaret has just charged into my office."

"Oh, oh," Grace laughed. "Bye bye."

Grace slipped her phone into her jeans pocket, stood up, and headed towards her mom's examining room, eager to tell her about her conversation with Sister. It was time for lunch anyway. Walking along towards the building, she spotted Jack on his way there for lunch, too.

"Jack," she called out, hoping to catch up with him. He looked somewhat damp, but not nearly as soaked as when they worked together over the dogs.

Seeing her, he stopped and waited for her to catch up. He looked so cute standing there, his head bent to one side, his clothes a mess, his hair in his eyes. She couldn't believe he was hers, well, maybe hers.

"Have you talked to anyone at Cat's?" she asked as she walked up to him, slowing a bit to appear unhurried and casual.

He put his arm around her and they continued walking, Grace trying to hold herself away from his soggy shirt, yet wanting to feel his arm around her.

"Yes, just talked to my dad," he said, looking down at her beside him. "You sure smell better than yesterday."

"You have no room to talk," she said, laughing. "You smell like someone who's been rolling in the mud with a collie or two."

"Dad says Mrs. Townsend is revving up for the book banning trial, and he hopes you will be allowed to speak. He figures you'll give a good defense of the book," Jack said.

"How can they not let me speak?" Grace asked, puzzled.

"Saint Cat's is not exactly a democracy."

"But surely Sister Joan will let me speak."

"Dad also said everyone is bent out of shape because Essence is missing. Left town in a van with some guy named Louis."

"I know. Sister Joan just called me to see if I had heard from her."

"Have you?"

"Nope."

GRACE
Journal
October 10, 2005

It's been a busy day with more developments back in Houston than here until late this afternoon so Sister Joan, I'll fill you in on the latest. After your phone call, we all had lunch, a letdown after last night's celebration, but good food just the same. Jack had talked to his dad, and my dad had called Mom so all we talked about was what could have happened to Essence. We agreed she must be headed back to New Orleans, and maybe if conditions were livable, that was the best thing for Essence. She had loved that song so much—the one about missing New Orleans. Maybe that was where her heart was.

After lunch, we went back to our stations and worked a couple more hours. It was really hot, and I needed a break for a drink so I picked up a bottle of water and went

NOLA Gals/Barbara J. Rebbeck

looking for Jack. I walked a bit until I saw him sitting under our favorite tree. He had his journal so I figured he must be working on his assignment. He told me he was supposed to write poetry about volunteering here. He really surprised me by saying he liked to write poems. Weird, huh, Sister? So I kind of crept up on him from behind and did that old corny thing of covering his eyes and asking him to guess who. So he laughed and told me to shut up and sit down as he was writing great poetry. I did as I was told, bursting with curiosity actually, struggling hard to hide it and act cool. So I sat quietly, looking out over the dog runs, watching the dogs playing. You'd hardly know how traumatized the dogs had been when they arrived. They had such resilience. I have really learned that word, resilience, since I came here. Everyone pulls together, and the dogs respond. It's as if they're grateful for what we do, for the showers, the medicines, the hugs. And they bounce back. And Sister, I know we both have cats. It'd break your heart to walk through the cat barns. It's so hard to get a cat adopted. Everyone wants dogs. The cats don't come back as easily. Some are very distant, keeping themselves apart, hiding up in the rafters. Others have made friends and roll and play together in the straw. The sick ones are still in cages or crates as their wounds heal. Essence to me is more like a damaged cat, hiding in Houston. That's why I think she'll do better back home in New Orleans.

Minutes passed and I fidgeted until finally Jack asked if I wanted him to read his masterpiece. It was a poem about a dog he'd just finished hosing down. He was quite a character he said. Old bag of bones had really touched his heart. So he cleared his throat and gave a funny reading of his poem. He even gave me a copy. Be still my heart! So here it is, copied into my journal just for you back there in Houston:

Stranger sits,
his mud hair matted and clinging,
his brown eyes begging for companionship,
his stitched paw scratching in the grass
in the hot Mississippi sun.
I hose him all over revealing
a soggy whitish fur
curling tight in the humid air,
ribs poking from a too-thin chest,
long ears bobbing as he pants,
standing, shaking off the water
from wobbly, spindly legs.
A poodle left for dead
in Katrina's wake,
survives.

Jack Lowe

Jack had hardly finished reading the poem to me when I began to put two and two together. Was it old George that I'd heard so much about? Heroic old George who had tried to save Mimmi by refusing to get into the rescue boat, insisting instead on leading the boat's skipper back to the white shotgun house? Could it be?

Jack and I tore over to the run where he'd taken the poodle. There he was, his face pushed up against the chain fence, panting as I approached him quietly, not wanting to scare him, calling out his name. He stood on his hind legs and began to bark as I reached over the fence to pet his puffy

NOLA Gals/Barbara J. Rebbeck

white head. "It's him," I shouted over the noise. "I know it's old George."

So, Sister, don't you think it's ironic that we've found George, but lost Essence?

P.S. Don't you think Jack rocks as a poet?

ESSENCE

The old van crawled into the French Quarter in New Orleans late in the day, its engine just about to overheat. Tumbling out of the van, hot and sweaty, they stood on the sidewalk in front of the old hotel, waiting for Louis to park. For once there was no problem finding a space as the streets and parking lots were far less crowded than usual. Essence looked around her. Things didn't seem as awful as she thought they'd be. Maybe there was hope for their old white house after all. Char huddled against her. Harold and Mrs. Beaudrie walked ahead.

"Lordy, that was a long, hot ride," Mrs. Beaudrie shouted back to the girls. "Praise God he guided us back home."

"Come on. Let's go in," Louis said, pointing to the door of the hotel. "Hotel Dieu," the old neon sign flashed. There seemed to be some damage from the winds, but no visible water lines on the walls from flooding. Some shutters from the old windows hung oddly at different angles to each other, and the iron railings on the balcony were bent as if someone had punched them in spots, but all in all, the venerable hotel looked livable if in need of a coat of paint.

"Mrs. Beaudrie, what does *Dieu* mean?" asked little Char.

"Why, child, 'Dieu' means, 'God.' Ain't that a sign that He has led us home?"

"Thank you, Jesus," Char said, nodding at the old building.

The girls didn't need a second invitation and were the first at the entrance, running ahead of the adults, backing off only when they struggled with the heavy oak door. Turning to Harold, Essence said, "Daddy, I can't move this big old door by myself. Help me."

"Yes, ma'am," Harold laughed, bowing as he pushed the door open and held it for the tired troop of travelers.

Louis led Essence and Mrs. Beaudrie to the front desk, gesturing for Harold and Char to follow. As they crossed the lobby, Mrs. Beaudrie gave it a quick inspection, taking in two worn green velvet couches placed opposite a fireplace. Above the carved oak mantel, a portrait of a beautifully-dressed southern belle seemed to be smiling back at her. She wore a hoop skirt dress which showed off a tiny waist. It was a deep crimson velvet with pink roses encircling the scoop neckline. Her dark hair ringed her face in curls, framing her blue eyes. Beneath the portrait the name and date, *Mrs. Laila Winthrop, 1860,* stood out in gold letters. Standing next to her, Harold said, "The year before the Civil War began."

"Hello," said the puzzled lady across the lobby, leaning over the counter, wondering what wind had blown this small group back into the city and into her hotel. They stood assembled on the worn purple paisley carpet, the rug perhaps once beautiful Mrs. Winthrop's idea of a fine Persian treasure. Its purpose now was more to cover worn floorboards than decorate them. The hotel had definitely aged along with the lady in the portrait.

"Mercy," the lady said, giving the group the once-over, "Where are you all from?"

Louis spoke up. "Why we're from New Orleans, honey. Just back from Kansas." They all nodded, heads bobbing up and down, knowing he was lying.

"Whatever for? Don't you know Katrina and Rita have pounded this city? The Big Easy is now The Big Empty," she continued, eying them suspiciously.

"We'll take our chances," said Mrs. Beaudrie, having taken an instant dislike to this lady. "You hoping your little vacation don't end?" she asked, bumping her hip against the counter, pulling Char to her side. She had spotted a plate of pralines and reached for one.

"Oh, Lord," Harold broke in, fearing another cat fight between women. "Are you open for business?"

"You got any money?" she asked, showing her teeth off in a wide smile, her lips coated with thick red lipstick.

"Now, honey," Louis broke in, his smile in competition, as wide as he could stretch it. "What's your name?" He reached out his hand to cover hers, seeing no rings.

Pulling her fingers out from under his in a slow withdrawal, she looked at him, her eyes bearing down on him, her fingers tracing her lips. "My name? They call me Jeannine, sugar."

"I'm about to go fetch a hose to cool you two off," Mrs. Beaudrie said, rolling her dark eyes. "Honey, you got a room or not?"

"You say one room for all of you? You got to be kidding me," Jeannine laughed. Now who are these two pretty young ladies?" She poked her hand at Essence, then Char.

Mrs. Beaudrie pulled Essence beside her, scrunching her next to Char. *A hard luck story might help*, she thought. "Why these poor sad girls lost their grandmere in the hurricane. Then they lost their old cat, Delilah. And if that ain't enough, they can't find their cousins. You ever heard such a sorry tale?" The lies came easy.

"Only 'bout a hundred a day since Katrina had her way with us," Jeannine said, yawning to emphasize her indifference to them all.

"Come on, sugar," Harold tried. "I can play a trumpet to wake the dead or calm the living. You need some entertainment for your guests?"

"A music man, huh? Most of them are no good," Jeannine said, equally unimpressed with Harold's talent. She came out from around the desk and walked to the window in a slow sashay. Both men followed her every move as she stood in the sunlight, smiling back at them, her tight blue dress skimming her trim body, her dark curly hair framing her heart-shaped face. Char poked Mrs. Beaudrie and pointed at her silver shoes.

"You like these shoes, sugar? You should see them dance," Jeannine laughed, moving her feet in a jive step, smiling at Harold.

"Good lord, you two," snapped Mrs. Beaudrie. "Stop acting so thirsty in front of these two young ladies. And you," she said, pointing her finger at Jeannine, "you got a room or not?"

"Well," Jeannine said, crossing back behind the desk, "just let me check."

Essence let out a big sigh having used up her patience. They were definitely on her last nerve. "This is stupid. Must be other hotels along the street." She yanked Char away from Mrs. Beaudrie and started towards the door.

"Just a minute. Yes, yes. I see a room here. Yes, a definite vacancy. You got cash? Credit cards aren't working."

Louis spoke up. "I got some cash. And I got strong arms to help get this place back in working order. I can start with that iron gate out there. And Gabriel here has his horn. You got a man here with you, honey?"

"I got me a man, but he's out looking for what he needs to fix that balcony above our heads," Jeannine said, pulling a registration card from a drawer. "Computers are down so I'll need you to fill out this card." She pushed it across the counter, not sure who would fill it out for her.

"I'll do that," said Louis.

"That'll be two hundred dollars for the first night."

"For a broken down hotel?" asked Mrs. Beaudrie. "No way."

"Twenty-five dollars. No more," said Louis, "and that includes these strong arms to help your man pick this mess up."

Essence plopped down on one of the old couches, afraid the bickering over money would never end. Char cuddled up next to her, ready to drop off to sleep in the comfy velvet.

"I'll put you all in a suite on the second floor. Elevators don't work," Jeannine said, waving towards the stairway. "You'll have to find your own food."

"Can I take a bath?" Essence asked, dreaming of a tub of suds as she stood up reaching out to Char.

"Yes, we do have water back on. Just go easy on the towels. It'd help if you share them."

"I suppose you want us all in the tub together?" Mrs. Beaudrie said, still unimpressed with her hostess as she herded the troop to the stairway. At least they had a roof over their heads, and a few days, hopefully, until the girls' mama found their hideout.

"Gabriel and Joseph," Jeannine called, after them, looking up and reading their names from the registry card, "do let me know what I can do for you."

"Likewise, ma'am," Louis grinned back.

"Be glad to play you a tune, honey," Harold added, dancing a few steps and playing air trumpet for her.

"*Mon Dieu*," Mrs. Beaudrie sighed, "we're surely in trouble now, girls. We done landed in the Bible with our new names. Surely the Lord can forgive us for hiding."

"You're all about to get on my last nerve," Essence warned.

GRACE

All the way home in the vet van, Grace had begun to plan her counterattack for the *Mockingbird* hearing. The closer they got to Houston, the more Grace just wanted to turn around and go back to Tylertown. This was going to be really hard. She preferred reliving the fun they'd had last night at the send-off party the other volunteers had thrown for them. She, Jack, and Doctor Mom had been the guests of honor at a cook-out. Jeff and the locals from McComb had pulled together another feast. They had all sat under the stars in the warm Mississippi night air, swapping more rescue tales as they gorged themselves on too, too good food. Life had seemed simple for the crew of slightly smelly but loyal volunteers, all united in their love of animals and their determination to right the wrongs of Katrina. The luscious fragrances of smoked sausage, barbecued pork and sweet potato pie filled the little grove of trees as they huddled and ate not far from the dog runs. That had been such a good night—one of the best of Grace's life. She had loved being so close to Jack, sitting side by side, laughing and stealing a kiss as the sun set, offering them cover from her mom. She had loved looking out over the bonfire at the faces she had come to love and admire in just two short weeks, seeing these smiles above the crackling orange sparks that shot into the air and fell back in embers to the ground. Her journal was rich with new personalities, new lives she had touched, new friends for life. Jeff, the director. Alice, the cook. All the data people. The dog run builders. The animal transporters. Jim and Dave, the other vets. She had admired her mom before, working with her at her office. She knew she was such a caring person, not just in her professional life, but as a mom, but now she had even more respect for her. Her anger at being sent to St. Cat's gone now, she would need to call on all the strength she had seen in her mom, now that Grace had taken on the challenge of defending this novel, an "unpleasant job" as Maudie would have said to Scout. Was she up to it? Could she do Miss Harper Lee justice?

Old George nuzzled Grace's neck, and then plopped back down beside her, his head in her lap, waking her from her daydream. When they had been unable to contact Essence, not knowing where she had gone, they had called her mama in Houston. She had thanked them for finding old George and asked them to bring him to Houston. Grace knew that secretly Mama must be hoping she could lure Essence and Char home to their fuzzy friend. And what was Mama's real name anyway? she wondered.

She looked over at Jack beside her. He was asleep, his mouth open, a bit of drool escaping. What was going to happen with him now? She had just turned fourteen in June, and he was actually a month younger than she. These two weeks had been a time to get to know each other in a quick and almost too-close way, with Mom watching not too far away. Now what? The kisses between them had been sweet, tired, and sweaty, Jack usually smelling like the dogs he bathed. He had certainly seen her at her worst physically, but perhaps at her best emotionally, committed soundly to a cause. Her mind went again to the stories of the parties at houses like the Townsends'. What would Jack want from her? Expect from her? She wondered how far Lindsey had gone with a boy. Not that Lindsey would ever confide in her again.

"Grace?" her mom called back to her from the front seat. "You seem far away. Anything on your mind?"

"Just wishing in a way we could turn around and go back," Grace said, speaking softly, afraid of waking up Jack.

"Yes, it was a great experience. One we'll never forget," Grace's mom answered, "I don't think I've met such a great group of people—you know, people with their heads on straight—since vet school."

"Now we have to go back and face this whole book thing," Grace said, stroking George's head.

"Grace, it's up to you how far you want to go with this," her mom said, the worry obvious in her voice.

"I have to," Grace said, "for Essence and Char."

"What?" asked Jack, half-awake, half-asleep, sitting up and looking around just as George landed a sloppy kiss on his chin. "Grace, get off me," he said.

Grace reached over and slapped him on the thigh, laughing. "Can't you tell my breath from George's?" she said.

"Not in front of your mom, sweetie," Jack said, shooting a fake disapproving glare at her.

"Get him, George," Grace said, reaching down to the floor for her journal.

"Grace," Jack said solemnly, "did I tell you the Astros are playing the Cardinals for the National League pennant?"

"Yes, Jack."

"Did I tell you for the first time in forty-four seasons they could make it to the World Series?"

"Yes, Jack, and that they have three home games starting tomorrow…"

"Yes, Grace after they split the first two games in St. Louis. Life is good."

Picking up her journal, she shook her head at Jack as he slumped back down asleep again in an instant, George dozing off too.

GRACE Journal
October 14, 2005

So Sister, we're on our way home. In my first entry I said there had been no major life lessons so far. Now two weeks later, here is my list of what I have learned and questions I have:

1. I can survive without make-up, blow dryer, and daily showers.
2. I don't like surviving without the above when living in a tent with my mom and new boyfriend.
3. I have seen sights and lived through experiences I never hope to see or live through again.
4. I love animals, especially wounded ones.
5. I love people, especially committed ones and even wounded ones.
6. Nature can be a horribly unpredictable ugly force.
7. Are God and nature the same force?

NOLA Gals/Barbara J. Rebbeck

8. What does it mean to be in relationships with parents, friends, teachers, boyfriends? Who can you trust and how do you figure that out?
9. What battles are worth fighting?
10. What unpleasant jobs am I here to do?
11. Books can change your life.

Maybe I'm lucky that at this point I have fewer questions than insights. Let's see what the next weeks bring. I am fortunate to have experienced Tylertown. I will never forget this experience. And so glad I read *Mockingbird*. Now let me put to good use the lessons I have learned there from everyone.

ESSENCE Letter
OCTOBER 20, 2005

Hi, Gracie! Bet you are surprised to hear from me. I know you get home first from school and get the mail so this letter can stay a secret between us. Please! We are staying in an old hotel that wasn't hurt too bad by Katrina. We are all in one suite that has a bathroom all its own. A nice lady runs the place with her husband. I can't tell you her name. She is fine and reminds me of Mama—but nicer. We all have fake names from the bible so God will forgive us some. I can't tell you them even though you're my friend, Mrs. Beaudrie says. And Char thinks we're all playing a game.

NOLA Gals/Barbara J. Rebbeck

Harold already got a job playing his horn in a bar down the street. Louis is working at fixing up this hotel and others. We get some money off the rent that way. Mrs. Beaudrie teaches us girls during the day. She says she don't want us to be dummies cuz of a hurricane that we had nothing to do with. So we do arithmetic and French with her. The nice lady lets us do the sums for her hotel budget. And we are reading the book, Night by Mr. Elie Wiesel that I brought from St. Catherine's. That's real scary about the Holocaust in Germany. I think that poor boy had it much worse than us. Mrs. Beaudrie says that book should make us feel better about all we still have.

I suppose Mama is having fits looking for us. I have nightmares of Mama stomping up and down the streets of Houston, her nursing home smock stuck to her sweaty body. She's looking high and low, swinging her purse, knocking on doors, hiding in bushes, riding buses, stopping strangers, just hoping to find her girls. That sharp tongue of hers must be spitting out truths to anyone who gets in her way. We left in the middle of the night, and Char cried most of the trip. Harold says you still can't get to our old white shotgun house. He reckons not much is left of it. What is left he says is probably all rotted and moldy from flooding from the levees breaking. I hope I never see it again. That would just be too sad. But at least

I have my freedom. I'm not behind sharp, poking wires in a concentration camp, wearing raggedy striped pajamas and starving like the poor people in *Night*.

I wonder where old George has gotten himself. When we go out walking, I'm always on the lookout for him. Maybe he's still over in the 9th Ward somewhere. We told her we lost our cat, Delilah so I wait until we get a ways from the hotel to start calling out George's name, hoping he'll hear. The hotel lady told us lots of men have been around telling stories of rescuing animals. Sometimes they stop in the bar where Harold plays and tell sad stories, but some happy ones, too about finding dogs and cats, even birds. Harold says he always tells them about George, but I don't know if he can describe him good enough cuz he never saw him in real life. He says it's okay to tell these men the truth about George cuz they are mostly getting so drunk at the time, they won't remember much.

I hope you are back home safe from Tylertown and back at school. I know you will talk about *Mockingbird* when Mrs. Townsend tries to get it banned. I can't believe Sister will let that be. That book is an important one, and I know the hatred still is out there, and I lived it cuz of my color. That's why as bad as this old city looks, and she sure needs a new coat of paint, I belong here.

NOLA Gals/Barbara J. Rebbeck

Please don't tell anyone you got this letter. We are fine, and I have my daddy. That's all.

Love, Essence

P.S. No one here knows I wrote to you. I trust you as my friend.

GRACE

Grace finished reading the letter, folded it, and put it back in the envelope. She could hear George barking from the poolhouse where he had spent the day in air-conditioned luxury. He was really no trouble as he was trained to feed himself. All you had to do was leave his bag of dry food open near him, and when he was hungry, he would bury his nose in the bag, retrieve a mouthful of pellets, drop them on the floor, and proceed to chew them a few at a time. *Good doggy,* thought Grace. And she was careful to keep her dainties out of his reach. She'd leave him out there for a bit still while she gave Idol some attention. Poor kitty had been acting weird since George had joined the family. She was always rubbing up against Grace's legs as if saying, "Hey, I'm little and cute. Some attention, please!"

When they had returned from Tylertown, they had called Essence's mom, and she'd come over for a joyful reunion with her pet, rolling on the floor, George lapping his tongue all over her face. Now she was trying to arrange for him to come and live

NOLA Gals/Barbara J. Rebbeck

with her at the nursing home. Grace's mom had long said that old people in senior homes greatly benefited from pets around. In fact, some dogs were trained just to be companions, kind of mascots for older folks in care. She was going to work with George to get him ready to join the seniors. She would just calm him down a little and get him to hold back his enthusiasm a bit.

"Idol," Grace called, "where are you?" She walked into the living room and collapsed on the couch, her mind heavy with this latest predicament. Idol came running and leapt onto the couch, her little nose nudging Grace's face. "So how's your day been?" Grace asked, pushing her down into her lap. "So Idol, we have a letter from Essence. A very secret letter. Now what should I do?" Idol looked up at her. She was such a sweet ball of whiteness. She would never lie, she seemed to be saying.

"But sometimes you just have to lie. For a friend."

Content, Idol closed her eyes and a slow, low purr filled Grace's heart.

"Okay. Just sleep, you sweet thing," Grace said. "You never lie."

It had been a good homecoming. They'd celebrated by going to the Astro games Saturday and Sunday. They had been guests of the Lowes in a corporate box. Grace couldn't help but make the comparison to the past days, sleeping on the floor in a sleeping bag, grimy and far from this luxury. Jack had told her to enjoy the food, the drinks, and the celebration of their favorite team because they had earned it. So she had returned to school today, a study in contrast: two days of celebration and everything she could have wanted, following two weeks of deprivation in service to a good cause. *And now this letter*, she thought, turning it over in her hand. She was happy to know Essence was back in New Orleans, and she seemed to be fine so could she justify keeping her secret from her mama and from her own parents. But Jack? This was a tough one. And one of those looming decisions that wanted to send Grace scurrying back to her childhood, playing Barbies on the patio, an occasional dunking of the dolls in the pool her worst sin. At least the Astros were winning. They were up three-to-one games now, and slowly the entire city of

Houston was beginning to believe they would make it to the Series. Jack's favorite player, Roger Clemens, The Rocket had signed a one-year deal with the Astros. Jack had explained to her that if they went all the way to the World Series this would be his sixth time playing in one.

"Yes, Idol," Grace said to her fluff of a cat, holding her up looking her squarely in the eyes, "Jack does love his baseball. Time to go get George." Standing up, she deposited Idol on the couch and headed for the French doors to the patio. Just as she reached the door, the phone rang on the kitchen counter. Turning back, she picked up the receiver. It was actually a cool antique phone, an old style brass.

"Grace?" a voice asked softly.

"Essence?"

"Yeah, it's me," the voice came quietly. "I just had to call to ask about George."

Grace slid the patio door open and held the phone up. On cue George began to bark loud enough to be heard all down the street, let alone on the phone.

Grace put the phone back up to her ear and said, "Did you hear?"

"Oh, lordy, it's true? It's old George?"

Grace could tell Essence was crying. "Yes, we found him at Tylertown. Jack had seen him before me and described him in a poem he wrote for his journal for school. He read me the poem, and I jumped up and said to show me that dog now. We ran over to the dog run where they kept the big dogs, and there he was poking his head out the fence. When I called out his name, he started jumping and prancing like a fine dog of true French descent," she said laughing, hoping to assure Essence.

"I can't believe it," Essence said. "So he's staying with you. Does Mama know?"

"Yes, in fact, she may take George to stay with her at the nursing home. My mom says having pets around really helps senior citizens find someone to love and get love back. Your mama promises to warn the old folks to hide their dainties."

Essence was crying more now but she laughed at the idea of George sniffing around for ancient undies. "That's good," she said, "Mama needs someone to love her, too. I hope she isn't stomping all over town cursing at Harold and her lost daughters. Please don't say I called, Gracie."

With that the line went dead, but not before Grace had jotted down the number from the caller ID. Now that she knew even more about where Essence was, even more guilt tugged at her. Yet Essence seemed okay, just sad. That assured her somewhat. She would distract herself by bringing in George and rehearsing her *Mockingbird* defense speech for both Idol and him. They were a tough audience, she laughed.

MAMA

Sometimes she thought her heart would break, or maybe it was long past broken. Just shriveled pieces of a heart, straining to beat, wondering why. She had studied every part of the body in nursing school, but a heart drawn on a medical text page had nothing to do with the real emotions of her heart. She lay in the narrow bed, surrounded by what was left of her world. Not much at all. There was a drawing Char had made of what was in her heart after Katrina struck that she had taped on the wall. A photo she had always carried in her purse of her mother and her two girls, now in a dollar store frame, sat on the bedside table. Three uniforms hung on the back of the door from a hook. Her sturdy white nursing shoes rested on the old chair. Old George was still asleep at the foot of her bed, lying across her own feet. Rousing herself, wiping the tears from her face, she pulled her feet free of George, stood up, straightened her spine, and headed for the shower, her only luxury. At least she had a private shower. She spent her days rousing seniors of all sizes and mental states and taking them for showers in the communal baths. It was exhausting physical work.

Stepping into the shower, she turned the faucet to hot, and stood, waiting the seconds for the spray of water to start its cleansing. She raised her face into the steady stream, mixing her tears with the rush of water, sobbing freely, knowing her crying would be hidden, at least muffled. She bowed her head, letting the water flow through her hair and down her back, bracing her hands against the stall wall, supporting herself as she had all her life. She had met Harold when she was such a young girl. He was twice her age. His trumpet had called to her from down the street where he lived alone, a lodger in a big house. It had begun innocently, her just stopping to chat to him as she walked by his porch every day. He worked evenings into the early mornings, playing his trumpet at a local club. He would play for her and talk about the tunes, and soon she was an expert on Satchmo and all his contemporaries. She'd move on home and sit on her porch, snapping beans for Mimmi, listening to the trumpet. It kept calling to her, thick as molasses, sending chills down her back. She was only sixteen, barely into high school. A "promising student" they called her. Her teachers said she should think about going to college, saying they could help her get scholarships to the nursing school right here in town. But she was listening to different voices and music consumed her. She dreamed of a different future. She dreamed of following her man with the trumpet wherever he went, wherever he played.

Harold stopped by the old white house one night. Mimmi had gone to a movie with a neighbor. Denzel Washington was her favorite. She never missed a movie of his. Harold had his trumpet with him and sat on the porch in front of the old window.

"You want to hear a tune?" he asked.

"Oh, yes," she replied.

And so it had gone from there. The inevitable happened, and at almost seventeen, she had found herself pregnant with Essence. She kept his secret, never telling anyone who the daddy was. And he had left town, playing his music all over the state. He'd told her this was no life for her and the baby. Mimmi had protected her, all the time knowing the truth in her heart. She had worked hard to raise her daughter, proud and fierce. With Mimmi's help she had graduated high school and gone on to do a two-year nursing program. They both loved their little lady, Essence. Later a lady at church had whispered her young cousin's bad mistake into Mimmi's ear. And Mimmi's soft heart had taken a second baby into the house, promising never to reveal just who the true mama was. And so Chardonnai came into the old white house.

Then one day Harold was standing on Mimmi's porch. Mimmi was against him moving into her shotgun house, but "Mama," as Harold now called her, was still charmed by his molasses music so in he came. He was there about six months until he got a better offer to play and off he went to lodge with Mrs. Beaudrie in the 7th Ward. Essence had been so little she couldn't have remembered him as a daddy. But with her heart shattered, Mama had stayed in the little house with Mimmi, doing fine at her nursing job. They were a family: Mimmi with her truths, Mama with her dancing shoes by night and her nursing shoes by day, Essence with her kindly nature, Char with her baby cries and sighs, and last of all, old George with his taste for dainties.

Smiling, she reached for the shower faucet, turned it off, and opened the glass door. She grabbed a towel from the rack and began to rub the beads of water from her caramel skin. Rubbing hard, she erased the pain, the shame, the guilt. Gazing into the mirror, she reached to wipe the mist away. A tall, thin, lady appeared. Not bad looking, her hair tightly curled in the humid air. Leaning into the mirror, she traced the puffiness under her eyes. For thirty-one, she was still okay. She would survive. She had lost her mother and now her two girls to Harold. But she would work and live here with George, bide her time, and then wage the war to get them back. She had to stay calm now. Harold was always on her last nerve as Mimmi would say. But Mimmi was gone. How she missed that old gal. The fight was hers alone.

Moving back into her bedroom, she could hear the metal carts clinking down the hallway, bringing the breakfast trays as she reached for her underwear hidden under her pillow from

George. She'd need to begin her rounds, taking vitals in about fifteen minutes. She'd found that George distracted, even soothed the patients, as she checked pulses and took blood pressure readings. "Come on, George," she laughed, "time to greet the day."

SISTER JOAN

Lindsey Townsend was pregnant. Sister Margaret had found her just a few days ago vomiting in the girls' bathroom. They had called Mrs. Townsend to school and spoken with her after a private session with Lindsey. She had been shocked to learn that her stepdaughter had been sexually active for some time now and that she had already taken a home pregnancy test herself with the help of her friend, Madison, in the school bathroom. "But she's only fourteen," her stepmom had protested. Then she had flown into a rage, blaming the books they were forced to read at St. Catherine's, screaming about Lindsey. Sister Joan had heard rumors of the parties at the Townsends, unchaperoned and wild. In health classes, they had done all they could to warn the girls, and the boys for that matter, of the consequences of their actions. It wasn't enough.

Now she would speak to Mr. Townsend on the phone. She waited for the ring and the pick-up by his secretary at his law firm. She quickly passed her on to Lindsey's father.

"Mr. Townsend," she began. "this is Sister Joan."

"Ah yes, Sister. You have really upset my wife."

"I'm sorry, but..."

"We sent our daughter to your school knowing you would protect her. But you have failed. Failed us miserably. Why, just the books you have the girls read are enough to ruin their lives."

"I'm sorry you feel that way, but we need to talk about Lindsey..."

"We need to talk about nothing. You will not see our daughter again at your school, but you will hear from us. Good day, Sister."

Sister Joan stared at the dead phone receiver in her hand and tears began to fill her eyes. Should she contact the first Mrs. Townsend? She had always seemed a reasonable woman. She decided to wait, to gather courage.

There had been other pregnant girls at St. Catherine's since Sister Joan had taken over as headmistress, but few this young. The father of this baby? Lindsey said it was not one of the boys here at Cat's, but a sixteen-year-old public school boy she had met during the summer at a pool party. She said they had *done it* in the pool because she had heard it would be safe because the chlorine stopped you getting pregnant. Where did they hear such nonsense? But at least that took Jack off the hook. She had heard the talk of the two of them before he had become a couple with Grace.

Mr. Townsend had made it clear that his wife wished to continue her assault on *To Kill a Mockingbird* scheduled for next week's monthly board meeting. As to the answer to Lindsey's *predicament* as he called it, that would be a family decision, thank you. "So butt out," Sister Joan had heard as his silent message to her.

Leaving her office in the early morning calm before the onslaught of students, she made her way to the chapel for morning mass. Father was just about to begin when she took her place in the front pew. A few early birds knelt, scattered in pews behind her. She had so much to pray for today. And another phone call to make.

GRACE

She knew she would speak next. She had practiced over and over again for the last week, her copy of the novel so worn it was in pieces. The Townsends had arrived with their lawyer causing buzz in the room. A lawyer with a lawyer. What chance did Grace have? The first Mrs. Townsend was not attending tonight. The lawyers sat in the first row to the left of the board table. The six board members sat there with legal pads provided for them to take notes if they so desired. Sister Joan sat at the end of the table on the right. All who had asked to speak filled the second row. There was a podium with a microphone facing the St. Cat's Board of Directors at an angle so the audience still could see the profile of the speaker. It was a cool night, the windows closed to the outside commotion. Grace, seated with her parents, Jack, and the Lowes, felt sweaty. She could feel a patch of moisture forming on her back as she waited. They had been surprised at the crunch of people waiting outside when they had arrived earlier. Reporters from local TV stations and newspapers had pushed at them, bright camera lights in their faces. So-called adults held up signs shouting *Kill That Mockingbird* and *Protect Our Girls*. Grace had fought back tears as her father hugged her close, propelling her forward into the school lobby. She heard the shouts and jeers aimed at her and strained to keep her head up, eyes straight ahead. Ms. Rodgers had found her and given her a big hug. "We can do this, Grace," she had said and left to find her seat.

Now she waited in the auditorium. Her mother gestured for her to take deep breaths, smiling encouragement. Jack passed her a bottle of water so her throat didn't get too dry before she spoke.

Sister Joan rose and spoke first, welcoming the crowd and begging for decorum and quiet so all could be heard as they spoke. Grace was glad the loud protestors who had been let in for the meeting seemed to show Sister Joan some respect, but still she dared not turn around and face any of them.

Sister Joan continued and introduced the board members. They each stood and then quickly sat again, anxious to begin what would prove to be a long evening. Then the Townsends' lawyer rose and spoke at length about the book and how it certainly could corrupt young readers. He read passages from the book, focusing on the trial and its lurid nature. *How dare these teachers allow, even encourage the innocent children of St. Catherine to read such "literature?" Why, there was no telling where reading such shocking behavior in books could lead these innocent girls.*

Grace had listened in shock, wondering how many of the adults had actually read the novel. And if so, just how many of them had totally missed the point. She began to see the novel itself as an innocent mockingbird that this crowd of Christians was intent on shooting, no matter what. And she couldn't help but imagine innocent Lindsey in the pool with her high school boyfriend. She certainly hadn't learned that behavior in the novel. Gossip was all over the school about her pregnancy. Grace had heard nothing from her former friend.

Ms. Rodgers rose to speak and walked to the podium. Calmly she began her defense of one of her favorite novels.

Grace stared intently at the six St. Catherine's board members, looking for reactions. Some hint of their feelings for or against the novel. She blinked in surprise as one by one they changed before her eyes into the townspeople of Maycomb in *To Kill a Mockingbird*. To the left no longer sat St. Cat's Miss Jacobs, but instead her face darkened and became the wise Calpurnia, the Finch family's cook. She leaned towards Grace and said, "Remember, it's not necessary to tell all you know. Keep it simple." Winking, she sat back quietly and became Miss Jacobs again.

Then, Mr. Peters, the next in line at the table, faded into old Mrs. Dubose rocking in her wicker chair, assailing her as always when she walked by, leaning towards her, rapping her cane on the table, shouting, "Grace, I showed you real courage by overcoming my morphine addiction before I died. Don't let that awful lawyer run me down in front of this crowd. You hear, you horrid girl?"

Suddenly Ms. Maudie appeared seated to the right of Mrs. Dubose. She had her gardening hat on until Mrs. Dubose literally pulled it off her head with a glare and slammed it onto the table. Ms. Maudie had her usual way of explaining adults as she said, "Remember, Grace, some people are put here in this school to do the unpleasant jobs no one else will do."

Next to her sat Dr. Bellows, but he was fading, too as slowly Mr. Dolphus Raymond from the book came into view. Grace recognized him at once in his shabby clothes, misunderstood as Maycomb's town drunk. He had placed his brown paper bag on the table. Grace knew it contained only a small bottle of coca cola, two straws protruding. He spoke, "Remember the secret I've told you: You children can understand what adults can't."

Scout sat in the chair next to him. Scout, only six years old. Ms. Maudie leaned forward and looked down the table at her. "Sit up straight, Jean Louis, and stop scratching at your collar. The dress is lovely."

And last at the table was Tom Robinson himself, back from the dead. He knew injustice as a black man in the south in 1932, convicted of a rape he didn't commit. "Free us ghosts, Grace. You can do it. Free the ghosts of Maycomb."

Grace looked back at the podium where Ms. Rodgers was finishing up her portrait of the novel. For just a moment Grace saw Atticus Finch, the courageous lawyer, just behind Ms. Rodgers as he turned to her, fumbling with his pocket watch, "Climb into their skins, Grace," he said. "You can save us all."

Ms. Rodgers finished and the crowd rewarded her with polite applause and even a cheer or two from students. Grace's father squeezed her arm and whispered, "Be yourself. You can't lose."

"Grace?" Sister Joan was calling her name, gesturing for her to take the stand.

Gulping, she rose, her knees shaking, her hand grasping her written script. Her father stood and hugged her, propelling her forward. She glanced back at Jack who smiled encouragement and gave her the thumbs up sign. She made her way to the front, trying to avoid looking out at the crowded room. Faces blurred before her and a buzz rose then fell as she reached the podium, settled her papers in front of her, and smiling over at her mother, began:

"When I was first assigned the novel *To Kill a Mockingbird*, I could have cared less about it. It was a typical assigned text that I would make my way through, probably reading summaries online, but actually reading very little of the book. Then Katrina blew into my life, and everything changed. I went to the Astrodome with my dad, Dr. Woodson, and looked into the eyes of the ghosts of New Orleans. Before me I saw played out the great themes of this novel, *To Kill a Mockingbird,* still relevant after forty-five years. I saw black people—poor black people—who had lost everything. I saw Tom Robinson, a man unjustly accused of a crime yet convicted just the same, all around me. Atticus tells his young daughter, Scout, to climb into the skins of others and walk around awhile and only then might you understand them. I have done that since August twenty-eighth when a hurricane blew a great city away. I have seen these survivors come into our school and become silent ghosts, tolerated at best, terrorized at worst.

"Again in the novel, Atticus tells his children it is a sin to kill a mockingbird for they do nothing but sing beautifully in their innocence. I suggest as a girl of fourteen, that if this book is banned from St. Catherine's curriculum, you will have done just what Atticus has warned against, for this novel is a beautiful mockingbird song composed by Miss Harper Lee.

"It has been said that the actions in this book are those of violence and rape. But who is actually guilty and innocent of these actions holds up a mirror to not only 1930s Macomb, but also today's New Orleans, and yes, even Houston.

"Atticus Finch is the heroic lawyer, charged with the impossible defense of an innocent black man for the rape of a white woman. He defends Tom Robinson for as he says, he could not face his children otherwise. He is the moral conscience of the town, as Ms. Maudie says, picking up and doing the unpleasant jobs no one else will do.

"Tonight I ask this board to save this novel. It has truly changed my life. It has been a beacon guiding me through dark days when Katrina first struck, when I was at the Astrodome, when Essence and Char LaFontaine came to live with us, when I went to Tylertown to volunteer with pet rescue operations. It is a great novel weaving universal themes of racial prejudice, parent and child relationships, courage in the face of adversity, empathy for others, the loss of innocence, and resilience. And tonight, let me finish by reading from this book a passage that occurs just after Tom Robinson is found guilty of a crime he didn't commit. Atticus, his lawyer, must face his children, Jem and Scout, with both the truth and injustice of the verdict.

It was Jem's turn to cry. His face was streaked with angry tears as we made our way through the cheerful crowd. "It ain't right," he muttered, all the way to the corner of the square where we found Atticus waiting. Atticus was standing under the street light looking as though nothing had happened: his vest was buttoned, his collar and tie were neatly in place, his watch-chain glistened, he was his impassive self.

"It ain't right, Atticus," said Jem.

NOLA Gals/Barbara J. Rebbeck

"No, son, it's not right."
We walked home...
"Atticus—" Jem said bleakly.
He turned in the doorway. "What, son?"
"How could they do it, how could they?"
"I don't know, but they did it. They've done it before and they did it tonight and they'll do it again and when they do it—seems that only children weep. Good night." (Lee, 243)

Grace stepped back from the podium and moved directly in front of the board members and said, "Please don't make us, the children of Saint Catherine, weep. Thank you for listening. Good night." Looking back at the crowd, she thought for a quick moment that she saw the shadowy figure of Boo Radley slip back behind the hallway door.

LINDSEY
Letter
November 15th, 2005

Dear Grace,

I suppose you never thought you would hear from me again. But here I am and writing to you by snail mail even. It's almost Thanksgiving. Can you believe it? I am staying with my grandparents (my real mom's parents) for a while in Arizona. It's kind of boring here—too many old people. And it's really hot. They don't have grass here on the lawns, just sculpted gravel. Weird. God knows what Christmas will look like here. Maybe green gravel.

I had to write and tell you I saw the videotape of the Cat's Board hearing on Mockingbird. You were awesome and made me realize I'd been really stupid about Essence and the other kids from New Orleans. That expensive lawyer my parents hired just didn't have the passion you had. I was so proud of you and so embarrassed that I had dumped you as a friend. My mom sent me the tape to show off her lawyer, not knowing I'd finally see your side of the story. If you have Essence's address, I'd like to write to her and apologize if she would even open a letter from me. And I'm so glad the girls at Cat's will get to keep reading that novel.

I know you have heard I'm pregnant. I'm out here hiding, trying to decide what to do. I get fatter every day. I have awful stretch marks. At first I threw up all the time, but it's better now. The worst part is my dad and stepmom have practically abandoned me. They say I have brought shame on the Townsend name. I hardly hear from them at all. But now I know who really loves me no matter what. My real mom. And maybe you, too? The baby's father is long gone, too. I won't even embarrass myself by telling you his name. He says he can't ruin his scholarship potential and his future university placement by having a baby. He actually called me a "liability." At least that's what the lawyer's letter said. He didn't know my mom is a lawyer, too. But she says we will have dignity and not ask for anything from that arrogant little so and so. My mom says she will be here for the delivery, and I am really scared about all that. And then I WILL be a mom. Me. Lindsey Townsend. Mom says it's up to me about what to do. So I have talked to people about maybe adopting out the baby. They say I may want to keep it. I have the option. But what will happen to me then? My life will be over. I'll be a mom at fifteen. I'm used to options like what shade of nail polish to wear, not babies. I'm a kid.

Please be careful with Jack. You don't want to end up in hiding like me with options.

I wish we could just be sitting by your pool, sneaking a drink. Those were our best days.

Love from your BFF,

Lindsey

BILLY
Letter
November 18, 2005

Dear Essence,

I am keeping your secret address on a paper in my shoe. I will never tell nobody. I got a stamp and envelope from my teacher cuz I told her I was sending one more letter to Katrina victims. She said I was a thoughtful young man. And I guess it's kind of true cuz you are a victim after all. So it's not too big a lie.

I am doing better in Mississippi and yes, I can still spell it still! We heard our house is all moldy and lost so we will stay here until there is new houses for us back home. I have made friends named Jimmy and Betty Sue. We are in the same class and live near so we can play at night. You said Grace was here a while to rescue pets and she even found old George. I had no way to get to see her and meet her and that made me sad. I'm glad you called and heard George bark at you on the phone.

NOLA Gals/Barbara J. Rebbeck

Well, I guess this gives me my stamp's worth. Write back if you can. Happy Thanksgiving!

Your friend,

Billy

GRACE
Letter
November 20, 2005

Dear Lindsey,

I have read and read again your letter, not sure of what to do. How can I trust you again when you betrayed me in so many ways? I guess being with Jack has made me realize how little I knew you. From the rainbow parties you thought I was too childish for to your prejudice against the NOLA gals, especially Essence and her little sister, I learned I didn't know you at all. When we started to grow up and left our Barbies behind, we left much more back there, too. Our friendship. So I have had to deal with that loss while I grappled with all the turmoil Katrina caused.

In the end after talking to many people including Mom and Dad, Sister Joan, Essence and even little Char, I have decided I just can't throw our childhood friendship away. We've grown

NOLA Gals/Barbara J. Rebbeck

up together at each other's homes, in each other's pools. We've broken rules together and eaten fast food together. We've prayed together and croaked at Sister Grenier together. Together. And now that you have broken the biggest rule of all and ended up "with child" as they say, I can't desert you. So, yes, I will try to forgive you and forget the past. Well, not all the past, just the bad parts.

So are you wearing those mama-to-be clothes yet? Do you have a baby bump yet? Send me a photo. I'm dying to see what you look like. I promise I won't show it to anyone, especially not Jack. Mom says you must be about four months along and probably not very big yet. You always were too skinny. My dad and mom send their love and Dr. Dad-to-the-rescue says he'll talk through your decisions with you if you like. Funny, I never thought you'd be one of his "loonies," I mean "patients!" They even suggested we might come visit you over winter break if it's okay with your grandparents.

Don't worry about me having to hide away pregnant. Mom and I had a really good talk about sex and Jack and me. I thought it would be super embarrassing, but Mom was pretty matter-of-fact. Maybe because of her dealings with animals. Anyway, we both agreed I'm too young to get too involved with Jack for now. But Mom says, if we stay together, I must be honest with her if I need to think about staying safe. She'll help me with choices, but she said she hopes this is years off. Jack is cool about it all. He's not the kind of guy to pressure me into anything I don't feel right about doing. It's not like I'm acting like a nun or anything, just knowing when to stop for now. I'm a kid!

So Happy Thanksgiving. This year I am grateful we are friends again. Take care of yourself and you better write back.

Your good friend,

Gracie

ESSENCE & GRACE

Essence and Grace had been writing back and forth for months now. As Christmas approached, Essence was becoming more and more excited. Grace had told her there was to be a Pet Reunion Fair sponsored by Best Friends at The District Garden Hotel in New Orleans from December 16-18. The rescue efforts had continued at Tylertown, and the exhaustive data collection had led to the idea of bringing more pets back to their owners, while at the same time welcoming back volunteers from the past months. So Grace was coming and soon. Their letters had updated them on each other's lives. She had all the details on Jack's favorite Astros losing the World Series to the Chicago White Sox in a sweep, giving Chicago their first title since 1917. She had rejoiced when *Mockingbird* had survived the witch trial of Mrs. Townsend. She had promised not to tell about Lindsey's pregnancy. She had promised not to tell how far Jack and Grace had gone in the pool house. She was relieved that Grace and her mom had had an honest, open talk about where her relationship with Jack was going sexually. No chlorine nonsense for her friend. But what she had been most happy about was getting back in touch with her mama. Grace had broken her promise, but Essence now knew sometimes that could be for the best. So when her mama had called Char and her on the phone at the hotel, she had stood first quietly, watching Char so happy to hear from Mama. Given her chance to talk, she had bubbled over, realizing just how much she had missed her mama. Jeannine laughed when they told her the truths about their lives and their real names. She said she had suspected something all along, but bit her tongue so's not to get them all in more trouble. Mrs. Beaudrie said it was more likely Jeannine wanted their money as paying customers were hard to come by after Katrina blew through New Orleans.

Now Essence was on her way in Louis' old van to the hotel with Harold and Char for the people and pet reunion.

"What is that noise?" Louis shouted, peering through the windshield.

The hot morning sun blurred his view enough that Char shouted out, "It's dogs—must be a million of them."

"And cats, too. And cages of birds," yelled Essence.

"You got that right," said Harold, looking out the side window from the backseat as Louis pulled up to the side lot. They parked and walked back around to the hotel entrance, very carefully weaving a path through the animals, some caged, some on leashes.

"Oh," said Char, "It's like a zoo. I want them all." She said, leaning over to pet a calico kitty.

"You know Jeannine says we can bring a cat back for the lobby. So start looking," Louis said, pushing Essence forward.

But Essence was not looking much at the animals even though they were hard to ignore. No, her eyes were scanning the crowd for Grace. It had been so long.

"I know. You're looking for Grace, but you got to help us find us a cat," Harold said, afraid to go back and face Jeannine without one. She'd been so good to them since they had arrived in October. They had moved into two suites now. And what he knew, but Essence and Char didn't, was that their mama was coming with Grace and her parents. She would have George with her. They had spoken several times on the phone and were getting along much better. He had a steady jazz job now, playing at a club and making good money. Trouble was there was no place to live still except for the hotel. He wasn't sure how Mama would get along with Jeannine. She did have a husband, but Mama knew from experience that didn't count for nothing.

"Mama?" Essence saw her first, and ran across the driveway to her. She was just getting out of the vet van.

"Essence, child? You come give your mama a big hug, and look who's here to slobber all over you." She moved forward quickly as George butted her from behind, trying to move her along. "And where's my baby, Char?"

"She's over there by Harold, picking out a cat for the hotel lobby," Essence said, almost lost behind George as he reared up on his hind legs, panting, all pink tongue and big ears

"Eaten any good underwear lately?" she laughed.

Then Grace crawled out from the backseat of the van, Jack and her mom not far behind. "I'll go park," said Dr. Woodson from the driver's seat. There were hugs all around after Grace saw that the surprise of Mama being with them was okay with Essence. How could she have objected to old George anyway?

Mama sauntered her Mama-sashay over to Harold and Char who had her back to her, petting a cat candidate. "Baby?" Mama said.

Recognizing the voice, Char turned and flew into her stooped mama's arms, almost knocking her over like an unruly pet. "Oh, Mama, why didn't you tell me you were coming?"

"I wanted to surprise my baby. Now look over there and see who else is here."

Char followed her mama's hand and began to run as fast as she could over to Grace and George. "George, you are alive!" she shouted. George did knock her down, flat on her back, spreading kisses all over her little face. Mama watched her giggling daughter and thought she'd never seen her so happy.

"Mama," Char said, her face stiffening into sudden seriousness as she stood up, leaving George rolling on the ground, "I have a box with Mimmi's remains. What will we do with them? Sister Joan, Harold and me scattered some at the school by the statue. Harold played the trumpet. It was a good goodbye for Mimmi."

"Oh, Char," Mama said, hugging both George and her at the same time, "thank you so much for honoring Mimmi. We'll decide what to do with the rest of the ashes. Maybe we could put Mimmi to rest in the Mississippi. Mimmi loved that old river so. Don't you worry about it now though."

Dr. Woodson approached from the parking lot and took in the reunion, smiling.

"Let's go inside so I can meet all these rescue legends I've heard about. Where's this Jeff?" he said.

The hotel lobby was a little easier to walk through. Signs led them into a big ballroom where smaller animals, mostly cats and birds in cages were housed. A big booth with a sign for the organization Best Friends was at the back of the room along the wall.

"A parrot," Essence shouted above the noise. "Let's get Jeannine a parrot."

Grace, Jack and her parents left the others to their choices and went back to the registration table. The table housed several computers, plates of pralines, water bottles, and bowls of purple, green, and silver Mardi Gras beads. As they approached, Jeff spotted them, hopped up and came around for hugs. "My, you smell much better," he said, "and if I'm not mistaken, Grace, you've taken a blow dryer to your hair. And I detect a bit of make-up on those gorgeous eyes of yours. None on yours, Jack," he laughed.

"But I have showered," Jack laughed, shaking Jeff's hand.

"So how goes it?" Grace's mom asked. "By the way, this is my husband, the other Dr. Woodson."

"Ah, yes, the shrink," he said. "I've heard tales about you."

"All good, I'm sure."

"You bet. You guys coming to the dinner tonight?" Jeff asked, hurrying things up, knowing he was needed back at the table.

"Sure, we'll see you there then," Grace waved, turning to find Essence again. Across the large room, she spotted them all. Harold, hanging back a little, unsure of his role but trying awfully hard, had corralled George. Char and Essence with their mama were picking out a bright lime parrot for the lobby. Hopefully, they would not also choose a big old cat that would eventually eat the parrot. Essence picked up Char in her arms and helped her offer the bird a cracker from the tray nearby. *They could still be a family*, Grace hoped. They had lost too much not to put together what they had left of their lives.

Hearing her name called, she looked back and she saw her mom and dad arm in arm as Jack hurried to catch up with her. "Let's go see all the New Orleans we can find," said Jack. "There's still so much to be done here. So much to be salvaged or rebuilt."

"You know, we could look into working with Habitat for Humanity, rebuilding houses over spring break," Mrs. Woodson said, already planning her next project in her mind.

"Great," Jack and Grace said at the same time, then looked at each other and laughed.

"Come on, NOLA gal and NOLA gent," her dad said, tossing purple and green beads to Grace and Jack. "Let's go. For now, it's party time. Let's find some good times in the Big Easy."

"At last," said Grace, looping the beads around her neck and grabbing Jack's hand. "Time for a parade. Time for some pleasant jobs." Mom began to sing loudly. That lazy river tune oozed its molasses path out across the room as they all joined in singing, happy to be in The Big Easy.

AFTERWORD

It has been my privilege over the years of my teaching career to introduce Maycomb County and the characters of *To Kill a Mockingbird* to hundreds of teens. In fact, currently seventy-five percent of American students read the novel at some point in school. It is also a novel that appears on many banned book lists. Writing my own novel, I reached back to those classes when I watched as my students became engrossed with life in the small southern town, only to be surprised and angry at the injustice Atticus Finch, a white attorney seeks to right by defending Tom Robinson, a Negro of a crime he did not commit. Atticus fails. As the verdict of guilty is read, his daughter, Scout (Jean Louise) is sitting with the blacks in the balcony, the only place they are allowed to sit in the segregated 1930s.

> ...Atticus put his hand on Tom's shoulder as he whispered. Atticus took his coat off the back of the chair and pulled it over his shoulder. Then he left the courtroom, but not by his usual exit. He must have wanted to go home the short way, because he walked quickly down the middle aisle toward the south exit. I followed the top of his head as he made his way to the door. He did not look up.
>
> Someone was punching me, but I was reluctant to take my eyes from the people below us, and from the image of Atticus's lonely walk down the aisle.
>
> "Miss Jean Louise?"
>
> I looked around. They were standing. All around us and in the balcony on the opposite wall, the Negroes were getting to their feet. Reverend Sykes's voice was as distant as Judge Taylor's:
>
> "Miss Jean Louise, stand up. Your father's passin'."
>
> (Lee, 241)

Reading that scene in the novel or seeing Gregory Peck take that walk as Atticus Finch in the movie always gives me chills as likewise my students were always moved. And so I sought to pay tribute to Harper Lee and her novel in my novel. I have been able to find a few of my students from years ago who are all ladies now. In the following reactions, they express the impact reading this book had on them as teens. So Miss Harper Lee, we stand for you as you pass by.

Reflections

Having grown up in a relatively homogeneous (read white) town, I had been naïve on the topic of racism. Reading *To Kill a Mockingbird* was an awakening to the subject matter as well as a lesson in the nature of people. It would be years before I would fully understand that this was not merely a fictional account, but a glimpse into our history as a nation and conflict that can arise even half a century later. To this day the story of Atticus Finch, his children and neighbors and Tom Robinson cause the hair on my arms to rise as I consider the lessons these characters learned and taught me as a schoolgirl.

JuliAnne Pardon Diesch

Sometimes I am bewildered by the close-minded, close-hearted people I see on the news or encounter in daily life. I wonder how it could be possible not to consider other points of view, when for me, it seems almost second nature to have a world view and moral code that involve being open and inclusive of everyone, to disdain prejudice, and to try to suspend judgment and understand where people are coming from. Simply put, to follow Atticus Finch's advice to "climb into a person's skin and walk around in it." Sometimes, it's easy to take for granted that I didn't burst forth into the world with such an enlightened perspective; I was guided by role models, including fictional adults—and the non-fictional grown-ups who introduced them to me. Reading *To Kill a Mockingbird* in 8th grade with Ms. Rebbeck meant learning about the world alongside Scout and her brother, Jem, discovering the dark side of our past (and current) history and humanity, and making a conscious decision to try to be *good*, whatever that meant.

And while learning history on its own is important, seeing it come to life in stories like *To Kill a Mockingbird* is incredibly powerful. Identifying with the characters and being right there with them makes it personal. Their experiences, their choices, their wonderings and wanderings and adventures and misadventures, their joy, their pain—it all contributes to developing a growing sense of morality from a young age. Jem and Scout and Atticus and Boo Radley and Tom Robinson crawled into my heart one cold winter night in 2001 and huddled up with me in my room as I read. They have stayed with me as I've grown up and continue to grow. They are part of the lens through which I see the world, and their story is a part of me.

Gina Sultan

Before reading *To Kill a Mockingbird* I was aware that it contained something important. That Atticus was a character to be admired. That closing its covers would pass me into the part of a population affected by Harper Lee's words. Reading *To Kill a Mockingbird* at 13 is something of a tradition, and I felt ready for its messages. I was in the 8th grade and I felt it was the first "real" novel I would read. It wouldn't condescend to my youth or dilute the hard truths of its content: The lesson that our systems can fail us. That we'll eventually understand and even fight the impulse to become reclusive. That our innocence will be lost along the way. Reading *To Kill a Mockingbird* at that age is in itself a loss of innocence. It is where we learn the creep of inequality and the complexity of compassion, the struggle of tolerance, and the wisdom that comes from watching someone else grow up while doing so ourselves.

Laila Aukee

I was first introduced to Harper Lee's *To Kill a Mockingbird* when I was a student in Barbara Rebbeck's 8th grade English class.

Years later, I still find myself transfixed by Maycomb, Alabama and the lessons on life that the characters of that "tired old town" taught me. I remember relating to the apprehension and curiosity that both Scout and Jem felt in regards to the reclusive figure of Boo Radley. I remember the electrifying shock that I felt when members of the jury convicted Tom Robinson of raping Mayella Ewell. The injustice haunted me, and just like Jem, I felt a deep sense of disappointment in the decision that was made; however, this disappointment was overshadowed by a sense of elation when Boo saved Scout from Bob Ewell's attack. The expansive range of emotions that the novel introduced us to was conducive to creating an experience that extended beyond the walls of the classroom. To this day, my heart aches for Tom Robinson's untimely demise and Boo Radley's life of solitude and seclusion.

By asking her students to read a novel that dealt with mature themes such as human morality and racial segregation, Ms. Rebbeck drew out the Scout character in all of us, encouraging us to question human nature and change our social perspectives. Much like Jem and Scout, our own perceptions of certain characters changed throughout the course of the novel and as a consequence, we changed too. Reading the novel as a class afforded us the ability to understand and unravel the assumptions that we made as readers. Nobody expected Boo to be the unsung hero, nor did anybody expect Jem's character to be called into question after Sheriff Tate discovered that he was responsible for killing Bob Ewell. Barbara Rebbeck used the teachings in the book to remind us that initial assumptions aren't always accurate, and that courage in the face of evil will always triumph, even if various forms of injustice occur. The lessons I learned in the 8th grade after reading *To Kill a Mockingbird* remained deeply engrained within my memory since they taught me about human dignity and respect, as well as compassion and kindness. I became a better person after reading that book, and for that I have Atticus, Scout, Jem, Boo and Ms. Barbara Rebbeck to thank.

Husnah Khan

SOURCES

Readers who are interested in learning more about Hurricane Katrina, other natural disasters, or great survival books and media and of course, *To Kill a Mockingbird* may consult the following references:

Music CDs:

Louis Armstrong: Greatest Hits. RCA Victor, 1996.

Goin'Home, A Tribute to Fats Domino. Vanguard Records, 2007.

NOLA. Harry Connick, Jr., Columbia Records, 2007.

Some Hearts. Carrie Underwood, Arista, 2005.

A Tale of God's Will, A Requiem for Katrina. Terence Blanchard, The Blue Note Label Group, 2007.

To Kill a Mockingbird. Elmer Bernstein, Varese Saraband Records, 1997

Movies:

All the King's Men. Columbia Pictures, 2006.

Animal Planet Heroes: Hurricane Reunions, Discovery Channel, 2006.

Animal Rescue Katrina. Studio Mythopoetika, 2006.

Beasts of the Southern Wild. Fox Searchlight, 2012.

Dark Water Rising. Shidog Films, 2006.

Hey, Boo: Harper Lee and To Kill a Mockingbird. First Run Features, 2011

Hurricane Katrina. WGBH, NOVA, 2005.

Hurricane on the Bayou. Image Entertainment, 2007.

Katrina's Children. Shadow Pictures, 2008.

To Kill a Mockingbird. Universal City, 1962.

When the Levees Broke, A Requiem in Four Acts. HBO, 2006.

Books:

Anderson, Allen and Linda. *Rescued, Saving Animals from Disaster.* New World Library, 2006.

Best Friends Animal Society. *Not Left Behind.* Yorkville Press, 2006.

Blom, Paul and Haueisen, Kathryn. *God in the Raging Waters.* Augsburg Fortress, 2006.

Brinkley, Douglas. *The Great Deluge.* HarperCollins, 2006.

Burke, James Lee. *Pegasus Descending.* Pocket Star Books, 2006.

Burke, James Lee. *The Tin Roof Blowdown.* Simon & Schuster, 2007.

CNN Reports. *Katrina, State of Emergency.* Lionheart Books, 2005.

Cooper, Anderson. *Dispatches from the Edge.* HarperCollins, 2006.

Deraniyagala, Sonali. *Wave.* Alfred A. Knopf, 2013.

Dyson, Michael Eric. *Come Hell or High Water.* Basic Civitas Books, 2005.

Frommer's *Texas.* 4th ed. Wiley Publishing, 2007.

Harris, Kendra Marie. *Nice Try, Katrina.* Infinity Publishing, 2006.

Hoog, Mark, ed. *Letters from Katrina.* Growing Field Books, 2007.

Kliman, Gilbert, M.D., Oklan, Edward, M.D., Wolfe, Harriet, M.D. and Kliman, Jodie, Ph.D. *My Personal Story about Hurricanes Katrina and Rita, A Guided Activity Workbook.* The Children's Psychological Health Center, 2005.

Kostro, Ed. *Through Katrina's Eyes.* Booklocker, 2006.

Lane, Julia Kamysz. *New Orleans for Dummies*, 4th ed. Wiley Publishing, 2007.

Lee, Harper. *To Kill a Mockingbird.* HarperPerennial, 1960.

McGrath, Barbara Barbieri. *The Storm.* Charlesbridge, 2006.

Mills, Marja. *The Mockingbird Next Door. Life with Harper Lee.* The Penguin Press, 2014.

Moon, Haley. *Katrina Tears.* Wasteland Press, 2007.

Murphy, Mary McDonagh. *Scout, Atticus & Boo.* HarperCollins Publishers, 2010.

Murray, Nancy H. *Gullah, the Nawleans Cat.* Hart Street Publishers, 2007.

Petry, Alice Hall, ed. *On Harper Lee.* The University of Tennessee Press, 2007.

Rose, Chris. *1 Dead in Attic.* Simon & Schuster, 2007.

Sepetys, Ruta. *Out of the Easy.* Philomel, 2013.

Shields, Charles J. *Mockingbird, A Portrait of Harper Lee.* Owl Books, 2007.

Smith, Sherri L. *Orleans.* Putnam, 2013.

Tarshis, Lauren. *I Survived Katrina, 2005.* Scholastic, 2011.

Thomas, Katie. *Waters Dark and Deep.* Cold Spring Press, 2005.

Time. *Hurricane Katrina.* Time, Inc, 2005.

Turnage, Sheila. *Three Times Lucky.* Dial, 2012.

Vidrine, T.L. *suffering katrina.* BookSurge, 2005.

Ward, Jesmyn. *Salvage the Bones.* Bloomsbury, 2011.

Warren, Robert Penn. *All the King's Men.* A Harvest Book, Harcourt, Inc., 1946.

ACKNOWLEDGEMENTS

I owe so much to so many, starting with my mom, Beatrice and dad, James whose comfy chairs were always surrounded by piles of books. Mom introduced me to Nancy Drew and Margaret Mitchell. My dad taught me British history. I cut my literary teeth on the six wives of Henry VIII. My parents took us to theater, concerts and operas, sparking a love for the arts in us all.

I also thank my teachers who inspired and taught me along the way. Miss Meyers who first thrilled me by giving me the teacher's edition of our third grade spelling book. Miss Downs who let me write and put on plays. And I am ever grateful to Vestal Hartwig, a tough southern lady who taught me to diagram sentences and write compositions and term papers back in junior high. She would have fit right in on the streets of Harper Lee's little town. Robert Rattray then smoothed my literary edges in Senior English. I also thank the E.M.U. French Department for demanding excellence and discipline from me.

As a teacher I learned as much as I taught. I thank the teachers who attended the Oakland Writing Project when I was its director. Mike and Angelle Batten, our OWP couple, and the irrepressible Sandy Riccardi and the very talented Sherri Masson. And hats off to our fearless leaders, Dr. Becky Rankin, Dr. Aaron Stander, Dr. Pete Rynders and Dr. Wilma Garcia, and our resident author, Stephen Dunning. and co-directors, Dr. Laura Schiller and Dr. Gloria Nixon-John. I also thank the teachers who I worked with over the years: Gary Williams, Carole Dawson, Linda Reagan, Armando Delicato, and Jim Ragland among others.

I thank the hundreds of students I have taught over the years. We always wrote together and many are still in touch and writing. Thank you to Laila, Gina, Husnah and JuliAnne for reaching back many years to share memories of reading *To Kill a Mockingbird*. Sister Bearss and Linda Schaffner of Sacred Heart know that I combined you two to become the kind-hearted, kids-come-first Sister Joan in my novel. She has a good, open heart like both of you do.

My family, or tribe as my mom called you, I thank you for all your support and love, especially my siblings and their spouses, Jan and Greg, Jim and Deb, and Carol and Jan. I also thank all my nieces and nephews, cousins, and the next generation of little tots and my biggest fan, Kevin. I greatly admire Bridgette, Sam, Ann and Ian who would make their dad, Dave so proud and Carol, Sue and Jeff, Deb and Keith, and Jeff and Elise who were the light of Mary, their mom's life. I also thank Mary, my sister-in-law for the loan of her poodle, George for my novel. He was too good a character to pass by. And I thank Karleigh, too for always saying thank you to me. Special thanks to Amy, my lawyer and Matt, my tech guy and Allie, fellow teacher. I thank Lisa and Kathy for listening and Larry Eby for sharing. And a super thanks goes to my always- welcoming British family, especially Auntie Jean as well as Judy and Neil, Paul and Martine, and David. My trips across the pond always rejuvenate me. And many thanks to my longtime friend, Yvonne and her band of women whose friendship contributed to the development of the New Orleans gals and taught me about "getting on people's last nerves." Thanks also to my writing group members, Tracy and Kristin. That hurricane extended metaphor gave you something to chew on. I thank you, Gloria, always there through good times and bad, for your careful reading and suggestions and your ability to listen and advise. And Pat, thanks for the quiet sun porch. And to the latest addition of my family, little Gracie-Willow, my white fuzzball cat with the gray tail, I honor you by naming you after the major character in my novel.

I also give a nod to my former supervising teacher, Betty Jones. Way back in 1970 when she watched me teach French she suggested I definitely write a book someday. Well, Mrs. Jones, here it is. I also thank my childhood piano teacher, Bernis Fox who actually fired me. She taught me one powerful lesson: practice!

I thank Neverland Publishing for taking the chance on a book for teens that has neither a vampire nor a post-apocalyptic setting although the aftermath of Katrina does come close. Thanks, Maggie for your prompt replies and belief in metaphors. Kudos to Donna and Joe for supporting small press publication.

I honor the children of New Orleans who struggled so as they were evacuated across the country. I hope your lives have in some way outlived the grief you suffered under the hands of incompetent adults.

And last of all, I thank Miss Harper Lee for giving us all the gift of *To Kill a Mockingbird* and changing my students' lives. Everybody rise for this lady.

ABOUT THE AUTHOR

Barbara J. Rebbeck is a teacher and writer who lives in Royal Oak, Michigan. She has degrees from Eastern Michigan University and Oakland University in French and English. She has published poetry, fiction and professional articles. She is a past-president of the Michigan Council of Teachers of English and a former Director of the Oakland Writing Project. She especially likes to get her students excited about writing about their own lives. Barb's father was born in London, England so she loves to visit there as often as possible. Her dad always said she was more British than he was. She has been to England for very special events such as the royal wedding of William and Catherine and the Queen's Jubilee where she could be found in the crowds along the streets. She has a huge collection of British royalty china and figurines from the era of Queen Victoria through little Prince George. She loves going to the theater and is also a movie buff. She is very interested in the history of her family; the Brits on her dad's side and the French on her mom's side. But her favorite time of all is spent with her many nieces and nephews. She recently adopted a little kitty named Gracie-Willow. Sound familiar? Yep, she named her after her character Grace, one of the NOLA Gals.

The real George.